My Brother
SEBASTIAN

by

Susannah Pope

Grosvenor House
Publishing Limited

This book is published by
Grosvenor House Publishing Ltd
28-30 High Street, Guildford, Surrey, GU1 3EL.
www.grosvenorhousepublishing.co.uk

A CIP record for this book
is available from the British Library

ISBN 978-1-78148-546-0

For those who believe in angels

I

My dream is always the same. I am sitting in a small cafe in St Mark's square in Venice, watching the world pass by. The square is empty of tourists apart from two priests, deep in conversation, on their way to mass. The sky is cloudless, the sun high and the heat intense. A pretty waitress brings me an espresso. She smiles down at me, her soft skin brushing my hand as she places it in front of me. Her eyes are as blue as the ocean; her hair shimmering black, tied back loosely with a white ribbon. She turns and walks away; her body flirting with me as she turns. I rise and follow her into the rear of the cafe. I gently extend my arm to touch her elbow, hoping that she will turn around. She does but it is not the pretty waitress standing there but my younger brother Sebastian, laughing hysterically. I then wake up.

Sebastian has schizophrenia, paranoid schizophrenia; diagnosed one year ago after he climbed onto his college roof proclaiming that God would make him an angel if he stepped off the ledge. The nightmare began here. After a long spell in hospital he was discharged into the care of our parents, people who were completely ill-prepared for the journey of my brother's dependency on them. His illness nearly ruined my parents' marriage and, for me, I lost the little brother that I had grown up with. I desperately wanted my little brother back, if only for a short time, and so it was that I made the decision for him to accompany me on an art tour to Florence. This trip would change our lives irrevocably.

But before this, we must start at the beginning. Sebastian wasn't like 'normal' children. Whereas I mixed with the neighbourhood kids, Sebastian sat at the side watching other children play football or ride their bikes.

He was never grubby, scuffed his shoes or climbed a tree. I got into mischief and was even suspended from my prep school, aged 11, for turning the classroom into a refuge for lost snails. The teachers could understand one or two snails but I had gathered a whole colony of around 200 which were climbing everywhere, leaving their sticky trail behind. At school Sebastian was aloof and always preoccupied. He never bought a friend home from school for tea, to play with or, later, to study with. At the age of 11 he became obsessed with astronomy after our father had bought him a telescope for his birthday. He begged our father to allow him to paint the solar system on his bedroom ceiling and he would lie hour upon hour on his bed, completely still, staring up at his universe. Nothing could break his concentration and I often joined him, lying there in silence.

Whereas I experienced all the rebellion and angst of adolescence, Sebastian never did. He had no friends and never left the house apart from going to school, of course, alone. My parents put it down to shyness and never questioned his peculiarities. Our father, who had grown up in a stuffy, unemotional household, thought that he would just grow out of it. Sebastian's intense study regime seemed to border on obsessive; as every school book was meticulously annotated, numbered and placed in alphabetical order in a neat pile underneath his window sill. Every pen was labelled with the subject he wrote with it. After returning from school he would disappear up to his bedroom and lock the door. Our mother, fearful of him going hungry, would leave his meals outside his door then return an hour later to collect the, more often than not, unfinished plate. A small light could be seen under his door at all hours and once, terribly curious, I got on all fours and peered under the door; all I could see was a shadow which seemed to be dancing. However he never listened to music, not that we could hear, or even watched television. If my parents saw him it was briefly between his room and the bathroom and he would mutter something inaudible before shutting the door behind him.

He studied religiously at all hours and any free time during school would be spent in the library. He was a straight A student, unlike me whose grades fluctuated throughout my school years. My parents were thrilled when Sebastian gained a place at Jesus College Cambridge University, my father's old college, to read Astrophysics. The whole of his revision period he stayed in his room. After the last A level examination he emerged from the confines of his room. I was shocked to find him severely underweight; his jawline was more pronounced and he had more than a couple of days of stubble on his chin. I too was a fan of the beard much to the displeasure of my girlfriend at the time. He looked and smelt like he needed a bath. As I did not live at home he was quite a horrifying sight. It took a lot of encouragement to persuade him to tidy himself up and when he did so he looked every bit the good looking boy that he was. He was graced with our mother's beautiful facial features: deep set eyes, long eyelashes, prominent cheekbones and a sculpted mouth; whereas I looked more like our father, a little more lived in and far older than my years.

I was pleased to hear that priority was given to first year students to be accommodated in the college so despite his solitary personality there would be students and others around if needed and he wouldn't be left to his own devices in some miserable bed sit. My father hoped that university would make him into a man and rid him of his incredible shyness and awkwardness. I must confess even at this time I had my reservations as to whether this would be the best for him as he was rigid in his living and university offered a more social as well as academic exploration of life. My university days were the happiest for me as I worked hard; cramming for final exams with vast amounts of coffee and digestive biscuits, left lingering by my roommate but also played hard. I participated in in-college activities and rag week. Every Friday I attended the college drinking club and was very proud of myself that I could down six pints of beer without throwing up in the nearest flowerbed on the way back to my room. I had a varied array of girlfriends over three years; in my first year was a hippie who was desperate to start her own commune, a Goth and a young lady who would talk through problems with her cat Mr Snuggle.

I studied Fine Art at Balliol College, Oxford, much to the annoyance of my father, and then went onto the Royal College of Art for my Master's degree. Sebastian and I had an aptitude, and indeed passion, for art despite neither parent having had any interest in the subject. Sebastian enjoyed renaissance art, like me, but also more experimental art such as Bosch and, in particular, Dali. Sebastian said he liked the fact that Dali was a nonconformist and a rebel against the art of his time and he was, as Dali himself proclaimed to be, a genius. Although I studied Fine Art I also loved to paint landscapes and would like nothing better than to sit alone and draw the incredible contours of the English countryside. If I could persuade Sebastian in the summer months we would drive down to Sussex to the coast where he would usually lie beside me lost in the patterns of the clouds as I painted until the sun went down. Painting was something that bonded us together as brothers and years later it would be my guide in developing an understanding of how his fragile mind worked and how I could eventually reach out to him under his terms.

I didn't enter Sebastian's room at home, alone and in the light until few days after he went to college when my mother had asked me to retrieve any clothes that needed washing. As I stepped through the door, the smell was overpowering but not nearly as much as the decoration on the walls. I had a mixture of emotion upon seeing those walls; I don't know if I was shocked, amused or even frightened. All three emotions seemed to come at me with such a force that I fumbled for somewhere to sit down. I think I even closed my eyes wishing that the explosion of craziness in his room had not happened.

Sebastian's bedroom walls were covered in articles from newspapers, about UFO's, angels and miracles, cut- outs from his beloved astronomy magazines; organic food labels and, often explicit, photos from men's magazines which were glued and stuck to everything. There was a large mirror on the back of the door that looked like shrine. Stuck with glue in the centre of the mirror was a copy of Verrocchio's Baptism of Christ; a renaissance painting which depicts Jesus standing in the river Jordan as John the Baptist anoints him. Two angels kneel at the side holding Christ's clothes as God's hands are releasing a dove. It never occurred to me until years later, viewing this painting with Sebastian in Florence, that Sebastian wanted to be cleansed; not just physically but spiritually and in order to do that he claimed that he had to be pure and devout. Even though our mother was Catholic, Sebastian and I never grew up in any particular religion. Conversely our father was an atheist which always made me wonder how our parents ever developed a strong opposing-religion relationship. I never gave much thought to a higher power until Sebastian's diagnosis. Watching Sebastian spiral into a world of his own and unable to function I sided with my father. Our parents never entered his room and never saw the extent of my brother's 'peculiarities', as they so quaintly called them. I expect our mother would have been shocked and my father angry or repulsed at the extent of the religious fervour displayed everywhere.

I tried several times to talk with our parents about my concerns for Sebastian, when he told us of his place at college, but my mother and father outwardly refused to believe that there would be any problem with this. At that particular time, Sebastian just appeared rather moody and sullen but not unlike any other adolescent with the normal mood swings. He was also able to converse with intelligence and even showed excitement about his university place. I confess that at the time of the exams I believed that he was just under enormous stress due to his rigid work ethic and I was just thankful to see that, although moody, his affect had lifted and his demeanour had changed. It was a few weeks before he set off for university that his behaviour began to become increasingly bizarre. Once again he would retire to his room; presumably to read and always in solitude. His personal hygiene, or lack of personal hygiene, was again a problem and I thought it strange that my mother didn't notice or seem care although I later found out that he was placing his clean clothes in the basket to be washed over and over again. I removed them couple of times I saw them but they ended straight back in the basket. Over the following months he would frequently look, and smell, like a tramp despite vigorous efforts to keep him clean.

The day to leave for Cambridge arrived too soon for Sebastian. That morning he sat at the breakfast table, unshaven, in stained pyjamas with unruly hair covering most of his face. He sat hunched over, as though he was terribly cold, and stared down at the food my mother put in front of him with a confused almost quizzical look, as if being asked to solve a complex maths problem. I had come home from my house in Sussex to give encouragement to Sebastian and support to our parents.

"All right Seb?" He lifted his head and smiled weakly at me. "All packed?" Again he just seemed to force a smile. The awkwardness of this family breakfast was just intense. I tried to cover it up by talking incessantly, trying to change the mood. "I was really nervous when I went to college but I met some great people who felt the same way. It just took a little time to acclimatise." I was trying my best to lighten his mood and make him understand that it was a big step but was well worth it. I looked to our parents for support but none was forthcoming. My father continued to read the paper as if there was nothing important happening or being said so, resigned to this fact, I continued munching my toast as our mother tried to coax Sebastian into eating something. He looked uncomfortable as our mother made a fuss over how she had made his favourite breakfast and that it would be such a waste if she had to feed it to the dog.

"You need to eat something. It is quite a long drive and I'm sure you will be hungry. You didn't eat much dinner last night. Do you feel unwell?" Bizarrely as she said this she looked at me, not him, seemingly somewhat afraid of his answer. She touched his hair which he quickly brushed off. "Father will make sure you get something on the way. Won't you Edward?"

Finally my father looked up from the paper and muttered something in response. Sebastian continued to scrutinise the food and began lifting items of it to look underneath. I sensed that he wanted the food but wasn't quite sure that it was okay to eat. After a few moments of investigation he scraped the chair back, stood up and looking at no-one in particular shouted, "I'm not hungry."

He then made a quick exit up the stairs and we heard his bedroom door slam. Mother just stared at me, unsure whether to go after him or stay. I was quick to remind her of how nerve wracking it is to leave home and start university and so she sat down next to me and nodded, quickly recovering from Sebastian's demonstration. Our mother, I believed, was a sensitive woman but having a hardnosed man as a husband, sadly, over time had rubbed off on her. She was not terribly maternal, change that to not at all maternal, and certainly not physically affectionate towards us as children. Sebastian found that the hardest. My interaction with other children ensured a long line of substitute mothers, all too willing to hug and kiss me and generally make a fuss of me. Despite Sebastian's reticence of being touched as a teenager now, back then he desperately craved it. If he had a bad dream, which he often did as a child, he would creep into my room and curl up on the bed beside me. Mother, too, naturally also needed reassurance occasionally and I was the one who obliged, as her husband was more concerned with his legal career and his own ego. I don't believe she was ever frightened by her husband but there was something about his coldness towards her, Sebastian and me that left me with a feeling of uneasiness and, I admit, anger.

Our father, oblivious, indicated to mother that his cup of coffee needed filling and just returned to his paper. Our father was not a man of many words either, despite being a barrister, and he would not show his emotions, or admit that he even had any, so Sebastian's departure and nervousness was no big affair. Father would often get angry with our mother when she seemed to be concerned about us. He didn't want his boys to turn soft. I believed she worried deep down about both of us, Sebastian in particular, but this feeling was never vented.

Our parents believed that there were hazards in the world for which we had to be prepared as much as we could be. Their positive belief system, or more correctly our father's belief system, was passed down throughout our childhood and teenage years. I worked reasonably hard at school and surprisingly was made a prefect, a class representative and ultimately head boy, despite my earlier indiscretion with the snails. Both of us were sent to a private boys' school, comprehensive schools were for the lower classes, as our father believed that we would become better citizens and would not be tempted by something as frivolous as girls. We had to work hard for what he paid for in school fees which he dutifully reminded us at the beginning of each term.

Sebastian worked harder than I but he was never made a prefect or given any position of responsibility. He was considered strange by his peers and by his teachers and he could often be found sitting alone in the science lab at break time and at lunchtime. Being four years his senior I had had my own worries about exams, college and, of course, girls. I had to look outside the school for feminine company, which I found at the local drama club. I was never good at the acting but I worked back stage and designed and painted the sets for each new play. I only acted once; I had a mere five lines yet froze with fright on the first night. Consequently I never trod the boards again.

When I left for Oxford I was nervous as hell but also terribly excited. I would finally be my own man. I was finally free of my parents and I yearned for that independence. Like most first years I had periods of homesickness but my friends usually pulled me out of any slump. I would go home for the Christmas holiday but would spend my summer holidays working in a bar in Oxford to cover my mammoth loan and the debts that I had accumulated over the first year. It was here that I met my beautiful girlfriend Sophia. She was at the same college and I would watch her pass by my window every day. I had rooms on the lower floor, overlooking the quad, and they were awfully handy when I used to make my way back to my room slightly, or very, inebriated and couldn't manage to place one foot in front of the other or keep my sense of equilibrium. She made my day brighter. She had cascading black hair, which stopped at her waist, and a body which would make most women envious. She was breath-taking to look at. My roommate Alan and I would just stand with our noses up against the window counting the minutes until she would pass. When I finally plucked up the courage to talk to her the next time she passed my window I leapt off my bed, dived out the door and charged after her. Sadly, I tripped over the mat near the entrance door and landed flat on my face practically at her feet. My ego bruised, I pulled myself off the ground; my nose pouring with blood. She gave an embarrassed giggle, quickly rummaged in her bag and produced a delicate pink handkerchief. She just stood beside me a vision of loveliness as my nose bled and my eyes watered. My nose was broken and very kindly she accompanied, an embarrassed, me to the hospital and stayed the 3 hour wait to see a doctor. Due to the painkillers I was given, I was a little more flirtatious than I normally would be and on the way back to college I boldly asked her out on a "first" second date and she accepted. Thankfully no accidents occurred, just a lovely quiet drink in a pub beside the river. We shared a house in our final year and remained together. Sophia is Italian and hails from a small town in northern Italy called Montepulciano. She works as an assistant curator at the British Museum and we own a flat in Highgate, local for Sophia's work, and also a small house in Sussex for my painting. Every summer we travel to Montepulciano to see her family.

I digress. I left it a few minutes before I went up to Sebastian's room.

"Make sure he has packed everything Benjamin. We don't want to keep sending things he's forgotten."

"Seb, I'm coming in." I pushed his door open, the room was fairly dark and I could not see the extent or content of his decor and saw three suitcases open on his bed. Sebastian stood stationary in the middle of his room eyes focused on the ceiling; the luminous painted planets really highlighted the wonder of the stars. I looked up too and could understand why he found peace lost in the painting of the vast universe. I was quite envious that he could stare for so long and stay so focused. He seemed a million miles away.

"Seb! Sebastian! Have you finished packing?"

"Oh yes; quite ready to go. I couldn't quite close my suitcase though. There must be excess energy trying to escape."

"Oh right. No worries, I sort that out for you." On the bed lay the three suitcases of varying size. I noticed his wardrobe was still full of hanging and folded clothes and neatly paired, exceptionally clean, shoes. I unlocked the largest case which seemed excessively heavy. It was completely full of astronomy magazines, some dating back to the 1960s. The second case contained his telescope and the third case, the case which he could not close, was completely empty. The lid was unable to close because of a small box of matches balancing precariously on the suitcase edge. I don't know what was going through my mind at this point and I realise now, with hindsight, that if I had done more then he wouldn't have gotten so deep into his psychosis. But I was too young and perhaps I thought, like our parents, that he would snap out of it and suddenly become an outstanding normal adult.

I started to lift out the magazines and put them to one side. Sebastian moved next to me and as soon as I placed one of them on the pile now on the floor he placed them back in the case. It was futile to keep up this act. It could well have been a comedy act although the climax was not very funny.

"Why haven't you packed your clothes? You're going to need clothes."

"I don't need them."

"Oh, so you have some other plan for clothes that I don't know about?"

"I will be taken care of."

"Well that's great but I still think we need to pack some."

By now Sebastian was more concentrated on a rather large spider which was slowly crawling across a dusty pile of old magazines. He reached out, grabbed it and then opened the palm of his hand, spellbound by the creature he held. I have always had a fear of spiders and to watch a large spider crawling over his hand made my heart start to race. Thankfully he carefully carried the spider over to the window and very gently let it go.

"I need the magazines, Benjamin."

"You don't need all of them. You can't wear them or use them as a toothbrush. We will have to leave the magazines." His face dropped and almost immediately I caved in. "Okay you can pack a few."

I started pulling his clothes out of the wardrobe and filling up his suitcase. I had no idea what I threw into the case as I thought he would help me but he sat down on his bed just staring at me with a quizzical expression on his face, like I was doing something out of the ordinary. Three suitcases were now packed with the essentials of student living; well at least I hoped they were.

"You need to get ready, get washed and dressed. You know how Dad hates it if we're late. He wants to leave at 9. I think I've packed everything you need. You may want to double check though."

Out of nowhere he began to cry. I was quickly by his side but he quickly shrugged off my attempt to put my arm around him so I just sat beside him, being of little or no comfort. As quickly as he started to cry it quickly stopped.

"What's the matter? Please tell me." His eyes however were focused at an empty dark corner of the room. It was a long drawn out stare. It was like he was a horse which had just suddenly seen something in the distance and had wide eyes and alert, forward pointed, ears. I saw nothing but there was something bothering him. Something I could not see or hear.

"Sebastian we are going in half an hour." I repacked his telescope in its protective cover and packed it in a small holdall. I also grabbed an alarm clock off the bedside table and a couple of books off the floor. I ushered him into the bathroom to shave and wash, laid out a set of clothes and a pair of trainers on his bed. I left him to change and went downstairs to find my parents. They were still sitting in the kitchen in silence having another cup of coffee. I was in two minds as to whether to tell them about his packing and odd behaviour but my mother would just worry, in her own internal way, and my father would get angry about Sebastian's lack of impulsion to get going and having shown an unmanly show of emotion. All I knew was that my brother was upset and I didn't know why.

"Time to get going Sebastian." I ran two at a time back up the stairs and found him dressed and sitting on the bed. The beard was still there but not as shaggy as Robinson Crusoe.

"Come on let's go."

We gathered his cases and I ushered him out of the room and took a deep breath. I glanced out the window and saw Father standing beside his car, his Bentley, his prize possession which he had valeted every week, drumming his fingers on the roof and jangling the car keys impatiently in his other hand. I would have liked to have accompanied him but my father didn't want me to as he believed it would be better for Sebastian, whatever that meant. My mother was saying her goodbyes as I stood and watched my father inspect a small mark on the bonnet of the car.

"Study hard; try and enjoy yourself; perhaps make a friend. Father has bought you a new phone and transferred money into your account. Be good won't you?" She pulled him into an awkward embrace which was quick and perfunctory. I watched with sadness as my brother clung onto her, reluctant to let go. "Don't be silly now. Off you go; make the most of this opportunity."

Sebastian didn't seem convinced by this as he still held tight. I could not understand why she could not hold him for a few seconds longer; he was her youngest child leaving home and both our parents could only muster a pathetic hug and banal conversation. As Sebastian got into the car he gave me a look of what can only be described as fear. There was so much I wanted to say to him to ease his mind but he looked like he was on the way to the gallows rather than university, somewhere you are supposed to have some of the happiest days of your life. But for him it was the dark shadow of a life to come.

"See you then. I'll visit you in a couple of weeks. I'm coming up for an art exhibition, so perhaps I can stay with you for a couple of days." I tried to remain as cheery as I could but nothing seemed to move him out of his seemingly sad, and what seemed to be, incredibly lonely place. He gave me a meek wave as they drove out of sight. I stood at my mother's side.

"He'll be okay; won't he Ben?"

"I'm sure he is just nervous. He will be just fine," I said with my fingers and toes crossed. "Remember what I was like when I first went to Uni?" I still remember it as though it was yesterday. I was unable to eat anything for days prior to leaving and I kept buying more and more books thinking that I was an intellectual and needed fifty books to prove it. I was also terribly excited but once I started to say my goodbyes the butterflies started and my heart began to pound. I was as scared but I can look back thankfully with smiles, wonderful memories and good humour. "He'll be just fine Mum; just fine."

To take my mind off of him, even for a short while, I suggested we go for a walk. We needed to take our dog, or as I should say Sebastian's dog, to the park. Sebastian had found a stray dog, German shepherd mix, tied to a tree in the park with no collar of ownership so Sebastian bought him home. Our mother was horrified at the mangy creature and one that was practically the size of a Shetland pony and ate as much too. After much arguing and tears from Sebastian, our father said we could keep hold of him only until the owners came forward. We had no name for him so Sebastian called him Cosmo. No one claimed him so he became ours and all of us have becoming physically fitter because of it.

We walked in silence, just enjoying the beautiful autumn day. There wasn't a soul around. I just enjoyed the splendour of such nature and I would have liked to have been able to sit and draw or paint for a few hours. Brown is never chosen as a favourite colour but, on placed in the opening. It was completely empty. I know I should have said something and I'm sorry. I just thought it was Seb, just being Seb I didn't...."

"What? This is just ridiculous."

"I know."

My mother sat, hands together on her lap, her face unreadable. My parents clearly had no understanding of what this incident meant; what it meant now and what it would mean in the future. "I packed his stuff for him. He just sat on the bed staring at me as I packed everything." I didn't mention that he started to cry as I knew my father wouldn't accept that behaviour, so I just kept it to myself.

"He must just have been anxious about leaving. He obviously had not packed and had not removed the cases previous contents. There is nothing to worry about. He seemed perfectly fine when I left him. There is nothing to worry about."

My mother brightened and tried to make light of the conversation, "He has never shown any interest in charity work before. I think it shows how caring he is. Doesn't it Benjamin?"

"Yeah, that must be it," I lied frustrated. My brother rang again later that evening, slightly less fraught than previously. My father promised him, in a stern tone, that he would transfer more money into his account on the condition that, no matter how tempting, he was not to lend or give his money away.

The next tearful and bizarre phone call came a few weeks later. Sebastian tried to explain to our father that he had missed all his lectures as he didn't know where to go. He had been there for 3 weeks. His neighbour Alex was also reading physics and would have gone to the same lecture theatre or classroom so it seemed unlikely. We could not believe that he had not been to at least one lecture since he arrived. Sebastian's rigid regime was based around study.

My mother spoke to him briefly and tried without success to alleviate his obvious anxiety and to get him to calmly explain what was upsetting him but nothing, it seemed, alleviated his distress. My father decided to ring the college and speak to his personal tutor. His tutor asked that my father come up to Cambridge speak to her in person as they were concerned about my brother's behaviour.

I was at home in Sussex, struggling over an article I was writing for The Guardian on uncovered gems of renaissance art, when my father rang. Sophia was in Egypt for a few days attending a lecture given at the Cairo Museum. So there was just me and our Persian cats, Sophocles and Socrates, who were not much company and who indeed preferred Sophia. My father told me of his conversation with Sebastian and with his college tutor and that he would be leaving for the college that afternoon and asked that I be with him. The break was more than welcome and I arrived at my parents' around lunchtime. My mother sat at the kitchen table fingers clenched around a mug of coffee. My father was pacing the room trying to make sense of the situation. My mother asked about my work and Sophia and our lives, trying desperately not to talk about Sebastian.

Lunchtime was incredibly awkward, each of us caught up in our own little world so I was grateful that we needed to get going pretty sharpish if we were going to see his tutor before the end of the day.

I hugged my mother tightly; I felt like she really wanted and needed it despite her outward appearance. The conversation on the drive was rather stilted and uncomfortable. My father pulled over at the first available service station, I knew he wanted to talk.

"What's going on with Sebastian, Benjamin? He has always been an odd boy, I know that, but I just do not understand what is going on."

"I just think that maybe Sebastian going to university may have been too soon for him."

"Are you saying that it is our fault?"

"No. Just that perhaps he's not ready for university yet."

"Are you saying that we pushed him into this? University is a natural stepping stone after school."

"He did it because it was what he thought you wanted. I don't think he knows what he wants. He wanted you to be proud of him. But you know he doesn't like crowds of people; he doesn't socialise, he will spend his time there alone and that does worry me."

"He just needs to knuckle down and work hard."

"Dad, he always works hard. That is all he does." I could feel the anger rising and my face changing to the colour red. "What if it becomes too much for him and becomes stressed or ill?"

"You managed. You stayed the course."

"I'm not Sebastian."

"Benjamin. Do not raise your voice to me." He was looking around us and people around us were staring.

"I liked getting drunk on a Friday nights. I liked partying, night clubbing in London and meeting girls. I also liked the lectures and I liked to study. University was good for me and good to me. That's not Sebastian, Dad."

"I'm not having a son of mine give it up after 3 weeks into the course. He will have to knuckle down and learn how to enjoy his time there."

"You don't learn how to enjoy yourself. He has to make a decision. If he does decide to quit it will be his choice. You can't make him stay there. You would be embarrassed about having a son who quits university wouldn't you?"

"That is not the issue here. He is at the finest university, it is an opportunity of a lifetime and I don't want him to waste it."

"Exactly; you don't want him to waste it."

I couldn't continue talking to him when I felt so angry and he was so deaf to what I was saying. We sat in silence. I looked around at the other people near us: a young couple were laughing and holding hands tightly across the table; an older couple sat in silence but were saying so much with their body language and there was a young couple with a small baby. The father, one presumes, held the baby high making it squeal with delight. Families who themselves, whilst enjoying these moments, had problems equal to our own.

It would be an hour or so before we reached Cambridge. The skies began to darken as we set off again and soon the heavens opened. A torrent of rain pushed us on while many others took refuge on the hard shoulder until the heavy rain passed.

Cambridge is such a beautiful city but today I was too focused on Sebastian to appreciate the fine architecture and buzz of student life. As with most town restrictions we frantically tried to find a parking space and one big enough to accommodate the Bentley. My father eventually found a space on a quiet road near the college and was praying that no traffic warden would find us and that his precious Bentley would not come under attack from birds or humans. It was only a short walk to the college and we made our enquiry at the Porter's office. Sebastian's tutor would meet us there. Minutes later, an elegant lady, in her thirties I guessed, met us there.

"Hello Mr Bradbury?"

"Yes and this is my eldest son Benjamin."

"I'm Susan Latimer, Sebastian's personal tutor. Thank you for coming. Please, let's go to my office." She led the way out into the courtyard. "Did you come far?"

My father was never one for small talk so I tried to field the questions as much as I could. "We live in Barnes, Richmond; just on the cusp of London. We got caught in the rain on the way here so apologies for our tardiness."

"It's this way, just up here on the left." She opened the door to her office and once in immediately put the kettle on. "Would you like tea? Coffee? Please sit down."

"No! No thank you. My son Sebastian?" my father said impatiently.

"Of course. Sebastian does not seem to be coping well here." She said quietly as she sat down with us.

"What do you mean not coping?"

She leant slightly forward. "I understood, from his neighbour who was with him when he phoned you, that he rang you rather upset that he didn't know where the lecture hall was. The thing is, Mr Bradbury, Sebastian has been present at every lecture and sits religiously in the front. I spoke to Professor Waterstone and he said Sebastian doesn't verbally contribute much but his work so far is insightful and well written, if not a little unconventional. There is no problem with his work. Yesterday he walked out half way through leaving his books, bag and his shoes on the seat. His neighbour came back from a class to find that Sebastian had locked himself in his room. He did not respond to his knocking or calling so he went back to his own room thinking he didn't want to be disturbed. Early this morning Sebastian was found by a proctor wandering aimlessly around the college barefoot. He was taken back to his room and now refuses to come out. We have no idea whether he is hurt, upset or anything. We thought it best if you came across. We have no idea how to deal with him. We have tried the options available to us. He's broken no rules or had an argument with anyone and in no way is he in trouble."

"Thank you for phoning, we will sort him out. He is quite an odd boy Ms Latimer, I can't deny that. He just needs a firm hand. Early university blues that's all. I can only apologise for my son's behaviour."

We followed Ms Latimer across the lawn to Sebastian's room. His curtains were pulled shut. A porter gave Ms Latimer the key in case we had to force our way in. My father knocked hard on his door. He looked livid and I could tell he was embarrassed at this situation.

"Sebastian. Open the door." No response. I did not think there would be. "Sebastian. Open this door immediately. Miss Latimer, are you sure he is in there?"

"Yes, his neighbour heard movement in there about one hour ago."

My father, now red in the face, knocked loudly, "Sebastian, this is your father. Get out here right now. I'm getting very angry speaking through a door to a silly child." Nothing my father was doing was making the situation better. Ms Latimer looked extremely uncomfortable as I'm sure this response was not what she expected from a concerned parent.

"Dad, let me try...... Sebastian, its Ben. Open the door will you. I want to talk to you. I haven't seen you in a few weeks. Let me in. Please." I expected him to answer at least but he didn't. "Let me have the key." The room was dark and I fumbled around until I found the light switch near the door. "I'm just putting on the light."

"No!"

"I can't see anything. Can I put on the desk light then?"

"No main light."

"No main light. Okay." I fumbled my way around the room, feeling for the desk and light, as if I were blind and was finding my way around a room for the very first time. I turned on the small work lamp on what seemed to be his desk. Sebastian was huddled on top of his bed peering through his closed curtains as if in anticipation of someone. He didn't look at me when I switched on the light. He was in his boxer shorts and had on socks and odd shoes. I felt something papery underfoot. I looked down and the whole floor was covered with newspaper, like you would use while protecting the floor from a puppy.

"Hi, Seb."

"Shush!"

"What is it?"

"They're coming. I must be prepared."

"Who is coming?"

"Shush!"

"Who are you talking about?"

He repeatedly looked out of the small gap in the curtains.

"Can I sit on your bed? I've been to the gym, trying to lose the extra pounds I've gained from being in Italy, and my legs are aching."

"They are coming. I must be ready."

"Well I can leave when your friends arrive. I'd like some time with you. Sebastian, look at me." I moved slowly towards him and gently placed my hands on the sides of his face. I turned him towards me. His eyes remained fixed towards the window "Look at me. Sebastian; look at me." He looked. I just wanted to pull him into a huge hug but I knew that was what he didn't want. I was at a loss not knowing what to do or what to say.

"What are you doing here? You shouldn't be here, they are coming for me. You have to save yourself."

"We're here to see you. People are worried about you. Dad is outside, he is worried about you too" He began to shiver, the window was wide open. "How long have you been sitting here?" I grabbed a blanket off of the floor and put it around his shoulders. He shrugged it off. "Who is coming?"

"They will be here soon."

"Who?"

"The people." He turned from me and peeped through the curtains. "I have to be ready."

"We're going out for a meal, we will be gone one hour at tops and you can come back here to keep watch. But you must get ready now okay?" I tried to find some clothes but I could hardly make out what was in his wardrobe.

"I need to turn the light on."

"No!" he shrieked and got off the bed and turned to face me. I fumbled around in his drawers and pulled out a pair of jeans, a t-shirt of some colour and grabbed a jacket hanging in the wardrobe. I physically pushed the clothes at him, "Get dressed Sebastian." I was becoming frustrated and my patience was beginning to wane. He held the jeans, frowning, like he was looking at a complex equation.

"Seb, the jeans!"

I crouched down and looked under his bed for his shoes or trainers but then remembered he was wearing shoes but as he stood before me I could see that they were odd and on the wrong feet.

"Change your shoes you have them on the wrong feet."

"Ben, what is happening in there?" yelled my father through the door.

"We're coming. He is just getting dressed."

"Okay are we ready? We are just getting some food and will be right back here. Nothing's going to happen to you; just dinner. You do still eat don't you?" The smell permeating off of him was overwhelming; I didn't know whether it was the clothes or body. I don't think he'd washed in days. Our father was a meticulous dresser and stickler for good hygiene; he never went without a shirt and tie even for the most casual occasion. He never had a moustache or beard and Seb and I definitely rebelled in that department. The first appearance of my facial hair made me feel like a man and I was loathe to shave it off. The headmaster of my school wrote to my parents outlining the school code regarding accepted gradients of facial hair. Since my release from school the beard has remained. Sebastian's hair and beard are almost indistinguishable.

My father and Ms Latimer were in deep conversation outside. Sebastian looked relatively normal in daylight despite the near dark he got changed in. Father just looked at him with what seemed to be disgust and tried to usher us out of the building quickly. As he thanked Ms Latimer for her help, I could see how embarrassed he was. He was angry at Sebastian but couldn't find the right words to express it.

"Sebastian, why did you lock yourself in your room? Your brother and I are here because your personal tutor rang me. I had to take a day off work and I'm right in the middle of an important case. Have you nothing to say to us?"

"I'm waiting for them to come. I needed to be inside to wait. It's too busy outside. I didn't hear the door. There is nothing wrong. I just need to be prepared." He seemed confident as he said this. "Why are you here?"

"I've already told you. Who's coming?" said my father furling his brow. I think he hoped that Sebastian had finally made some friends.

"The people of course!" He laughed like we were being stupid for not knowing. Sebastian walked on ahead, so totally unlike the huddled boy that I found in the room.

I told my father that this was a conversation we had had already had and that he seemed upset about their imminent 'arrival'. I suggested that for convenience we find a restaurant nearby. Sebastian was quiet and didn't offer much in conversation. We found a small, half full restaurant near the college and were given a table next to a window. Sebastian seemed nervous about this, hesitating momentarily before he decided where he wanted to sit. His eye contact with us was minimal as he seemed preoccupied, his attention drawn to outside throughout the meal. My father was unsure of what to say or do initially and every few minutes that passed by would look to me for some sort of support.

"How are the lectures? Your tutor told us that you were very keen, it's just what I expect from you." Sebastian looked at me and I gave him a nod of encouragement to answer.

"Okay I suppose."

"Just okay? You go to one of the finest universities with the best dons and it is just okay?"

My father's gaze was fixed on Sebastian, waiting for more than his simple answer. I could see we were not going to get anywhere and I knew my father wouldn't bring up the fact that he had worried everyone, angered him and that now he seemed totally preoccupied and disinterested. It was as if it never happened. My father just carried on pressing the point about the greatest university ever. The harshness of him seemed woefully evident as he could not admit that Sebastian had a problem with which he could not and would not deal with. I watched closely as Sebastian fidgeted in his seat and looked again out the window with expectancy.

"Dad, it has only been a few weeks. He just needs time to settle down. He is just finding his feet."

"What about your friends? The boy Alex or whatever his name is?"

"He's been taken by the people. He is not coming back." My father assumed that he had been sent down despite Ms Latimer mentioning him earlier. He directed his answer out of the window rather than to my father's face. "I have to look out for them. Otherwise I may be punished."

"No-one's going to punish you, you are talking rubbish."

We ate in silence. My father ordered a double whisky, a rare occurrence, so I assumed I would be driving us home. I'm sure my father was completely confounded by the situation and I sensed also shame that it had come to this. Sebastian managed to get through the meal with some sort of semblance of normality but continued to look distant and barely spoke. He played with his food, dividing it into equal size sections on the plate.

"Not hungry Sebastian or are you just going to make pretty pictures on your plate?"

"Yes." He said to his plate rather than looking at our father.

I wished the meal would just finish, it seemed endless but my father repeatedly quizzed him about the content of his lectures and his friends or lack of. Sebastian seemed to drift off after a short while inspecting the far corner of the room with great concern.

"I would like to go now," blurted Sebastian as my father was in full flow about his university days. Both of us were sick of hearing about his college days and his lauded academic achievement. They were expectations that neither of us would be able to meet.

"Sebastian, do not be so rude, interrupting like that."

"Dad, I think we should go now too," I agreed." It was becoming more intolerable as the minutes passed. Sebastian rose from his seat and stood at the door desperate for a quick exit. I left my father to pay. "We will walk on Dad."

"Fine"

Sebastian was already ahead of me. I followed closely behind him and back to the college and back to his room.

My father was issued with a parking ticket which made my day, I couldn't help but smile, he was fuming of course, blaming me; blaming Sebastian; blaming the tutor for bringing him up to Cambridge; blaming everyone but himself. I felt sure he would want to challenge it in court or add it to his expenses. I took the wheel and we set off in silence for home. I'd left Sebastian a little happier; he seemed more comfortable in the confines of his room. He had asked about our mother and why did she not come too. I lied and said that she was ill with flu and didn't want him to catch anything. I could see the disappointment on his face but this was thankfully short lived. I stayed only for a few minutes as I felt our father's patience had run out. I was just glad that Seb was in brighter spirits and I could selfishly go home, feeling a sense of relief rather than guilt.

The journey home was long and tiresome as we were stuck in a traffic jam on the motorway for over an hour due to a loose horse which had escaped from a nearby field. It was a magnificent animal, black and white. It seemed like he was putting on a show for the drivers of the cars, teasing them as he trotted back and forth. His incredible mane reached his shoulders and, as the breeze lifted it, it moved like small waves in the sea. His triumphant body moved gracefully but powerfully as two hapless citizens tried to coral it until the police came. The spectacle came to an end when the owner, I presume, came to retrieve him. The horse gradually submitted to the actions of the owner and was trotted away following a trail of carrots. My father read a paper that was in the front of the car while this beautiful creature had put on a show. I would have liked to have escaped the confines and stuffiness of the car and him.

It was too late to travel down too Sussex so I remained at my parents' house. My mother asked whether he was behaving himself or was he in trouble and to be honest I didn't quite know either. We had no clue that this incident would instigate the rapid decline of the mental state of Sebastian. I too was at this stage in denial and all too optimistic that he would gradually return to a more normal state; a normal state for Sebastian that is. My father did not talk to me or my mother of the conversation with his tutor or about how we had waited outside his room as I had had to coax him out. It was obvious he wanted to forget that it had ever happened.

When my parents had gone to bed, I went into Sebastian's room; they of course had never been in there. Our Portuguese cleaning lady had gone in there once and refused to go in there again. She claimed to have seen some devil worship in there but she was a little bit crazy anyway so my parents just ignored her. I swear I saw her once making the sign of the cross outside his door. Once the main light had been turned on I saw the real extent of his deep obsessions. I felt like I was in some parallel universe. There was not one inch of wall space left. His collages did however cover the dreadful colour of magnolia and you were hard pressed to find any spec of it left.

Two walls were covered with articles on space travel and astronomy, huge posters of the solar system were overlapping each other and stuck to these were pictures of the space shuttles, super novae (stars exploding), balls of gas and fire and other astronomical phenomena.

These walls just seemed to reflect a teenage fanatic's interest in space and it didn't seem an unhealthy interest; in fact I stood and marvelled at the incredible photos taken from the Hubble space telescope. There were awe-inspiring pictures of the moon and other planets. Underneath most of the pictures were handwritten notes describing in great detail the co-ordinates of the star or planet in the universe in relation to Earth. I never understood physics, complex mathematical equations or any astronomical technicalities but Sebastian was their slave. Several of the notes referenced time travel and it appeared that he believed that this was possible through channels of energy.

On his book shelf were several copies of Stephen Hawking's 'Brief History in Time', all in pristine condition. A large note was pinned to the books which said "Time is not measurable and therefore irrelevant." An alarm clock which I thought I had packed into Sebastian's case was left on the floor and the face had been covered over with black tape, as was his watch which had been left on a shelf. Time had stopped in Sebastian's room.

Sebastian used to say that it made him feel very small as he looked up into space. Small and insignificant he described it and he would constantly question why people, like me, believed that there was no other life forms out there in the cosmos and that surely we, as humans, cannot be as naive to think that we on Earth are the only ones out there. I used to laugh, mocking him gently, at his conviction in such matters and tell him that he had been watching too much science fiction on television but he would reply that I would just have to wait as they are coming. They, I assumed, were the extraterrestrials he was so convinced about. I used to laugh at the sheer absurdity of it.

Displayed on the wall behind the bed was an eclectic range of religious paintings. The picture directly above his bed, I recognised immediately, it was a picture of Christ's crucifixion by the German painter Grunewald painted in the 1500. It's one of the most disturbing and meticulously detailed depictions of the crucifixion, and unlike other depictions, Christ's palms are pointed upwards and his fingers splayed up towards God as his body was cloaked downwards in agony. I was, and indeed always am, moved by the emotion of this work but it certainly did not belong on the wall, overlooking the bed of a teenager. It's a painting of anguish and that very anguish would be evident in Sebastian as the months passed.

Two other paintings caught my eye as they were paintings of Saint Sebastian, a martyr, killed by several arrows piercing his heart and neck. Saint Sebastian was bound to a wooden plinth with his hands tied, raised above his head, the position often mistaken for the body of Jesus. The other painting was similar but numerous arrows had pierced the body. I wondered initially whether he had chosen these because of their shared name but the theme of martyrdom became clearly evident as I continued the journey into his religious abyss. The whole wall was overwhelming with the theme of punishment and the suffering bearing down heavily upon me. Our Catholicism evidently weighed heavily on Sebastian, more so than on our mother and me. Peeking from underneath the bed was a large bible which he had been given by our devout grandmother. Mine was in a box somewhere in the attic gathering dust along with my rosary and other childhood things, stored and forgotten. Sebastian's bible was open at the Book of Mark chapter 9 v 47, which was highlighted in bright yellow. The familiar passage read:

"And if thine eye offends thee, pluck it out. It is better for you to enter the Kingdom Of God with one eye, than having two eyes to be cast into hell fire."

It meant nothing to me, just words, but it wasn't the only passage that I noticed that he had highlighted when I took the bible to bed later to look through. I continued to look around and I hesitated a moment beside his set of drawers surprisingly a little nervous of what I may find. The top drawer was locked but a small key was protruding under the lamp. Hesitantly I reached out my hand with the key but suddenly pulled it back just seconds away from committing a huge invasion of his privacy. My curiosity however was stronger than my sense of self restraint. I was hoping that the drawer just contained underwear or socks. Everyone keeps their undies in the top drawer. It did, but underneath the clothing were journals, what seemed like hundreds of journals. On the cover of the journals was his name, his full name: Sebastian Tristan Mark Bradbury and printed on the bottom right hand corner was some sort of coding in gold pen. The first code was NPOEBZ26BQOJ, the next journal, rather than B or No 2 as you would might expect, it read UVFTEBZ2713BQOS. The journal front covers were all encrypted. It was just like Sebastian to be so secretive but hundreds of entries themselves were not. There were no dates, no times, no other distinguishing features you would expect to find in a journal or diary. There were literally thousands of pages of meticulously neat handwriting from cover to cover. It was getting too late to start reading them there and then so I just grabbed a few at random, closed and then locked the drawer. I had no idea why I did that, I think I felt like a guilty parent who has just found their child's diary stuffed under a mattress and hoped that no one would know I had been in there.

Before I turned out the light while in bed later I searched his bible for underlined or highlighted entries. There seemed more highlighted passages than not. Bible study was never a big thing for me and learning even the basics I found hard going. I couldn't understand what most of these passages meant but the friendliness of Google would no doubt inform me in the morning. Other than that I'd need to see a priest. "Forgive me father for I have sinned, it's been ten years since my last confession and oh by the way could you just explain all these readings." Not a road I really wanted to go down.

Once in bed I began to read the first journal I had taken from the drawer. It may have been the first written, it may not. It described a dream, a daylight dream as he called it, which I assumed he just meant he was daydreaming like we all do. He described in vivid detail a black hole opening up in the sky and a ball of fire speeding towards him. The ball stops inches away from his face and a pair of huge hands appear and push him to the ground. The hands disappear and the ball of fire retracts through the black hole. He looks down at his hands, they are severely burnt but the peeling flesh exposes fresh skin. He then ceases to dream.

Initially it read like some sort of comic book story, starring an indestructible hero who ultimately saves the world from imminent disaster, but as I read on this dream would reappear time after time, never progressing from the original description or resolving any conflict or issue. It stopped dead always at that same point.

Interspersed with his dreams were concerns about the secret intelligence service, MI6, and how they could track him down by using implants and a special dye in his clothing. I knew he liked the James Bond series of books and thought that he was perhaps writing his own stories, although I know now that this was incredibly naïve of me, but it was impossible to comprehend why he would believe such a thing. As I was fascinated, yet fairly disturbed, by these entries; I could not help but read on. However this came to a grinding halt when the following pages were encrypted. It seemed like I had indeed stumbled on the first journal and that half way through he changed into code. There was no rhyme or reason for the code and I had no way of deciphering it. The other journals were exactly the same, the first 20 pages or so were in plain English and then the remainder of entries encrypted. I presumed the others in the drawer would be as well and I was disappointed, but somewhat relieved, by the fact that I would not get to read all his inner most thoughts and feelings. He wanted most of the entries to remain private and so in the morning I returned the journals to their rightful place under lock and key, believing that he had left them because nobody but could read them. But they disturbed me, disturbed me greatly and I wanted to know more about this world he was living in.

I returned to Sussex and I did guiltily take several more of the journals with me despite my self-restraint the night before and to a phone call from Sophia. She explained excitably that another relic had been dug up and that she had been invited to accompany the team on the dig where it was found. She was very passionate about her work, as was I, and I felt no compunction to get upset that she would be away for another week, even if it was for an old fossil. We'd been together for about three years now and time away from each other was not a new concept. Perhaps people are right thinking that time away made relationships stronger and I believed we were happy and content the way things were. The only bone of contention between us was Sophia's mother was an Italian matriarch who ran the roost of her four adult children. She somewhat frightened me; as did initially were Sophia's three brothers: Roberto, Marko and Stephan who reminded me of the brothers in the Godfather films. This feeling was, of course, misplaced and I grew to love them in my own way. Sophia is the youngest and very protected by her family. They disliked her decision to live in England but fortunately didn't seem to have a problem with me or have expressed any dislike for me.

Sophia's mother rang that evening expecting to speak to Sophia. I had to utilise my best Italian as her mother doesn't speak English. I was up to my eyes in paint as I was transferring my studio to another part of the house when she rang. The receiver is still splattered with a burnt orange colour which clashes with the white decor of the whole front room.

"Ciao, Benjamin."

"Ciao, Maria e bellisimo parlare con te. So Sofia e in egitto sta facendo degu scaui archeologici. Sono rimasto da solo con il gatto." It was extremely hard for me to try and translate the word archaeological dig without making a fool out of myself. I could have been saying anything but I ploughed on regardless, "Sofia lavora molto!"

"Quando tu e Sophia verrette a visitarci, papa vi mostrera I suoi vini?" The family had a vineyard and I had become very accustomed to the taste its wine.

"Come e stat il battesimo di Matieo? Io Sofia spervamo di poterci essere ma sforunamente sono dovito restare con mio fratello. Commucque questa estate auremo occasione di vedere tutta la famiglia."

"Il prete assaggio il vino si durante il battesimo Il prete assiaggio il vino e incomincio a perdere il controllo cosi Roberto presse il prette e lo porto a casa."

"Come sta tuo fratello Sebastian?"

Sophia's mother always asked about Sebastian even though none of the family had ever met him. "Sebastian e ok co vedo spesso, sta facendo l'universita. Verremo a visitarti presto."

I always needed a drink after talking to Sophia's mother as my brain always worked in overdrive trying to translate in my head and then respond appropriately. Languages were never my strong point at school and I always had a feeling of dread when Sophia was not there and her mother calls. I'm giving myself a few more years to perfect my pronunciation, if not decades. Due to work commitments we were unable to attend her nephew Mattieo's baptism which her mother and brothers were upset about. I know she would like to have gone but we were planning a trip to Montepulciano in the summer of the next year.

I took a bath, poured myself a medicinal whisky and settled down in front of the fire to read. The journals at first could be seen as some sort of diary but in truth were far from it. In the entries I could read he described himself as a slave, a slave to God and to the people, but it seemed he was also a slave to his own thoughts and mortality. As the journals were not dated it was impossible to say how long ago the entries were written. There were numerous entries about his daylight dream and countless references to demons, hell, purgatory and violent death. The text read like word vomit, spewing forth the most intense horrific thoughts imaginable. I read on until self-preservation told me to stop. I wished I could have deciphered the encryption and read all the entries however I didn't think my brain would have been able to handle anymore.

For some inexplicable reason after digesting these, I sat in the bath fully clothed and let the water run over me. Perhaps I needed to be cleansed of what I had just read and needed something real to awaken my own sense of mortality. After the ritual ducking, I tried the college phone and his new mobile which my father had reluctantly bought and sent him and of course it went to message. I left a quick message for him to ring me and that I hoped he was okay, but I doubted that he would ring me back. I tried the college pay phone several times throughout the day but nobody answered. I thought of ringing our parents but I knew it would be a futile exercise so I made the decision to drive to Cambridge in the morning and make a surprise visit. I would also swing by our parents and pick up Cosmo as I knew Sebastian would prefer to see him than me.

Both my parents were out so I let myself in, with the key that was placed under a garden ornament for emergency purposes, and left a note in the kitchen explaining that I had taken the dog with me to visit Sebastian and I would return him later that day. I had tried to ring my father earlier but typically his phone was switched off. I arrived in Cambridge early in the afternoon and, after four attempts at parallel parking into a space small enough for a bicycle. I took Cosmo for a walk and grabbed a sandwich before walking to the college.

As I approached the college I could see some kind of commotion. A large crowd, of what I presumed were students, was gathered in the quadrant all with heads looking up towards the roof of the building. I couldn't make out what they were looking at so curious I naturally walked a little quicker. I thought it maybe some students pulling a stunt like a college friend of mine, who used to sunbathe naked on his college roof; I could never figure out how he could ever have such balance to remain there until he was burnt to a crisp.

As the scene came more into focus, I saw that it was Sebastian's building and that not only were students there but also the police and an ambulance. My immediate thought was Sebastian and I began to run; Cosmo raced ahead and pulled me ever quicker into the fray. I pulled up short; I could see clearly the naked form of Sebastian balancing precariously on the roof arms spread wide. I forced my way through the crowd to the front and saw Ms Latimer at the door talking to the police. I forged ahead wrought with panic.

"Ms Latimer. Benjamin Bradbury, Sebastian's brother. We met a couple of weeks ago."

"Mr Bradbury we've been trying to contact your parents." I checked my phone; I had switched it to silent. "Your brother has been up there for, I believe, nearly an hour. We cannot talk him into coming down. He hasn't made any significant moves to jump but no-one yet has established contact with him. Two students walking back from class spotted him; they thought it was just a prank. He was up there at least half an hour before they reported it."

"What's being done to bring him down? Who is up there with him?"

"Nobody at the moment. He climbed out of a small window to get up there and his door is locked; it's not easy to get up to the roof. They have to find an entrance other than the window so officers can get to him."

"Has something happened to make him do this?"

"Not that we know off. He remains a quiet student who you don't really hear about. His neighbour Alex sees him at lectures and he didn't think that there was anything particularly unusual. We've kept an eye out for him after your last visit but everything seemed to be going fine."

"Well it's obvious that it's not; isn't it? Why is no-one doing anything? Everyone is just standing around."

I was full of questions but just desperately wanted to get to him. I heard a sudden gasp by the crowd and looked up. He had moved slightly further towards the edge of the roof but still no action was forthcoming. I still had a hold of Cosmo who was now thankfully lying quietly at my feet. Two police officers, who looked barely my age, approached Ms Latimer who then introduced me.

"Where do you reside Mr Bradbury?"

"What's that got to do with this? You're asking me my personal details when my kid brother is balancing on a roof ledge completely naked. Aren't your priorities wrong? I want to go and speak to my brother."

"I'm sorry Sir we have to wait until the right personnel arrive and we can't let anyone up there."

"He's my brother for Christ's sake. Surely it's up to me if I want to risk life and limb going up there?" I wasn't making any headway and only seemed to be making waves and enemy of the teen police.

"Sir, we cannot let you go up there. We have to wait until......."

"...the correct personnel arrive. I get it; but who exactly are we waiting for?"

"The fire brigade is on its way and a police physician. I understand it's frustrating but we'll get him down. Just calm yourself down sir."

I just thought 'patronizing little twerp' but thankfully my brain over ruled my mouth. Within minutes of this conversation a fire engine arrived and the police officers with me went to liaise with them. Ms Latimer stayed with me which provided no comfort whatsoever. It seemed like a new millennium before the fire officers found a way of reaching the roof. Ms Latimer was talking about God knows what as I had drifted into a parallel universe of sunshine and smiles where this situation was definitely not happening.

I stood, barely listening to her as Sebastian teetered on the edge of that roof. I blame myself of course for not doing something sooner but that is the crux of hindsight. I still blame myself. But there he was and I had done nothing to prevent it from happening. Sebastian was drawing even more of a crowd and I could see his delusion of being Jesus and the Sermon on the Mount. Some people were jeering encouraging him to jump while others just stared with their mouths open like guppy fish. After a few minutes I saw an officer standing on the roof a good few feet away from Sebastian trying to coax him down. We couldn't hear what was being said but it didn't seem to be working.

Ten long minutes had passed when the officer retreated but he was back up there though a few minutes later accompanied by a man in a dark suit. I presumed this was the police doctor. Cosmo now started to get irritable and was moving in and out of people's feet. Very kindly Ms Latimer offered to take him back to her rooms, Cosmo jumped at this offer with alacrity as did I. I couldn't stand all this waiting around, the sheer impotence of the situation. I gathered all the balls a guy can muster and headed over to the police officers.

"Look, I could have got my brother down from there 20 minutes ago. You don't seem to be having much luck so let me go up there and talk to him. He'll listen to me." I think I began to beg at this point, "Please just let me talk to him." The officers looked at each other as if they all shared one brain and had to make a collective decision.

"You can't go up there alone; we'll need someone to go with you." Thank God for that, even though I was required to wait until they found a fireman to escort me up there, at my own risk, of course. I was never good with heights and even now I never walk up the stairs in high rise buildings anywhere near the windows. I had a sudden thought about our parents and that I had failed even to ring them. Our father naturally would be in court prosecuting some idiot for their pure stupidity. While I waited to go up I rang him, he was just about to go into court. I didn't beat around the bush.

"There's been an incident at the college with Sebastian. He climbed onto the roof of his dorm building."

"What a stupid boy. You'll have to ring me back; I'm just going into court. We'll talk about it then."

"Dad you don't understand. The police, fire service, doctors are all here. This is a major problem, more than a major problem, Dad."

"Benjamin, you'll just have to deal with it as best as you can until I speak with you later. I must go. No doubt he's just playing some silly game."

It was typical of him; family always took second place. I was in two minds as to whether to ring my mother as I thought perhaps she would be worried but I'm sure but, like our father, she would no doubt be immune to our troubles and not very good at dealing with such a situation. A few moments later I was escorted through a maze of small steps up to the roof. I could feel my pulse starting to race, whether this was due to the height or the impending situation I was never sure. I could hear a man's voice trying to coax Sebastian off the ledge; it would take more than just 'come on son, come down' to get him down but it was a valiant effort under the circumstances nonetheless.

The roof top; I was going to either pass out or vomit from the height I was sure of it. The police officer didn't look too comfortable either as he stood rigid rooted to the spot. The doctor, a youthful specimen, stayed well back and it clearly looked like he hadn't done much of this before. The officer came over to me, glad of a respite from the front line.

"Sir"

"I'm Ben Bradbury. Sebastian's brother. Has he said anything or asked for anything or anyone?" I was living in false hope that he would ask for me.

"No and he is just not budging. He's very close to the edge; we are reluctant to press him into anything." He looked over to where Sebastian was. I couldn't see him from where I was standing so I tentatively moved out so I could. I could see Sebastian's pale, naked and thin form from the back. He was standing, as the officer rightly described, possibly only inches away from the ledge. His arms were open wide like a bird in flight and his head was tilted back. He reminded me later of Icarus in Breughel's painting 'The Fall of Icarus'.

I made a cautious move towards him, carefully planning my steps so as not to startle him or cause me to fall. "Sebastian," I called out, firstly in just a little more than a whisper. As I sadly expected there was no response from him. I tried again a little louder this time and again no response. I was absolute that I would not leave that roof unless he was with me and that I would stay hours if I had to.

"Sebastian. It's Ben." Could he hear me? I couldn't tell but I continued on trying not to show the pure desperation in my voice. "What are you doing up here? It's very dangerous and I'm worried that you might fall. I don't want to come to close as you know what I'm like with heights. Remember when we stole that window cleaner's ladder as children and I fell off and broke my arm." I saw a flicker of body movement and he tilted his head sideways towards me. He looked puzzled as if he was struggling with recognition. "It's me, Ben."

Finally he spoke, "That's nice, but I don't know you Ben."

"I'm your brother."

"Everyone is my brother; everyone. Do you know how many stars there are Ben?"

"No. How many are there?"

"Around 400 billion; in our galaxy of course. It equates to the number of grains of sand on the earth. Humans are just specks of sand and it is the stars who own the universe."

"I didn't know that. Perhaps you could tell me more about that inside. We could look at your astronomy books and you could show me."

"I can't show you in a book, Ben. We need to be out here and wait until the sunsets and the magical time begins. I must wait here for that time."

"For what to happen?"

"To become an angel of course. God has chosen me to be an angel. I'll be able to fly to the stars with my own wings." He faced forward again, flapping his arms gently up and down as if ready to take flight. I exchanged a glance with the others, he was completely away with the fairies; he had to be off this roof immediately. I pursued the astronomy angle hoping to keep his mind occupied.

"Can't you become an angel inside?"

"Don't be silly. How am I going to take off inside?"

"What if doesn't happen today? You can come away from the ledge and we can sit and wait; we can keep watch out the window. I've bought Cosmo to see you; he's in the car waiting for you to take him for a walk."

"Cosmo?"

"Our dog; your dog. Remember you found him in the park?"

"Dogs are the hounds of hell, they are slaves to Satan, so I would never have a dog."

I took another tentative step towards him. My legs were shaking so much as I was precariously getting closer to the edge of the roof.

"You must be so cold. Aren't you cold Sebastian without any clothes?"

"Why do you call me that name?"

"What would you like me to call you?"

"My name is irrelevant now but you will find out soon enough, unless the others find me of course."

"Who is going to find you?"

He bowed his head. His arms must have been so tired but he stood stoic in his position. I was getting more scared and cold as the minutes passed as I just wanted this to be over and my brother by my side, safe. I felt completely useless now as I was making no positive progress. I was somewhat embarrassed that I had made such a fuss to get up there but I couldn't help him or them in any way.

"Look how the disciples have gathered below. They are waiting for this momentous occasion where we can all see the wonder of his work. Look how they have torn off all their shackles of material wealth."

I knew that the only people gathered below were unkempt hung over students and nosey onlookers; the same normal onlookers who gawp at traffic accidents on motorways. I was getting more and more despondent with every passing minute as I watched and listened to the sad spectacle of my deluded little brother. I then had a desperate thought.

"Hey Seb, I'd like to hear about becoming an angel. Do you think I could become one?"

"If it is part of God's plan."

"I think it is, but I'd like to know everything about it before I become one. How can I become like you?"

He turned around and faced me. "Would you?"

"Absolutely. But I need you to come over here to tell me as it's too near the edge for me. Could you do that?" I could see the full extent of his scrawny body. He had too big a layer of skin covering his bones. His face was gaunt, not helped by the mess of the beard covering it. I held out my hand to him, it too was now shaking uncontrollably. "Take my hand and come away from the edge. It will make me feel better if we aren't too close to it." He paused for what seemed like an eternity and then shuffled his feet a little and moved a cautious foot in my direction. "Take my hand. It's okay it's just a little cold as I'm sure you are." He put his other foot cautiously in front in readiness to move. "Come to me." He shuffled over to me like he was about 80 years old afraid to make a sudden movement. He reached out his hand to mine, pausing a few agonising seconds before finally touching it. It felt good and I just kept on squeezing it as if I never wanted to let him go. I'd never gotten physically close to Sebastian as he always balked at affection such as hugging, apart from those from our mother that is. I reached out to embrace him and to my relief he allowed me to hug him and I held on to him tightly. "Good boy Seb. Good boy," patting his back as he then lay limp in my arms.

One of the officers handed me a blanket to cover him. He was ice cold under my touch. There was a huge feeling of relief up there on that roof. The officers paused and kept their distance until we were ready to go down. Sebastian now looked rather confused as people were fussing over him, well, me fussing over him. He never said another word to me until days later. The doctor who was present came over to us and gave me the bad news.

"We will take him from here."

"Take him where?"

"We need to take him to hospital for assessment. You can accompany him if you wish. He won't be staying here I'm afraid."

"Where will you take him?"

"Hitherbrook Psychiatric Hospital; it's just outside Cambridge. Let's get your brother into the ambulance and we can take it from there, okay?"

I nodded compliantly. We took Sebastian down the stairs, shrouded in a blanket, and out into the spectators' arena towards the awaiting ambulance. I felt like we were convicted felons on our way to prison from my father's court. I was glad in a way that Sebastian was too much into his own world to even notice the gawping, as if he was an animal in a cage, but I noticed it and I tried, with every breath and every step I took, to drown out the sound and remove the crowd from my line of vision. I wanted my brother's dignity to remain intact. Ms Latimer caught us before we climbed in the ambulance and told me that Cosmo was in her office and she had a friend who lived locally that would happily keep him overnight. In the midst of everything I had forgotten about the poor dog. The doctor managed to persuade Sebastian to lie down for the journey and I couldn't help but be a mother hen, clucking around him ensuring that he was alright. His eyes were wide open but he didn't look frightened, just confused. That of course would change over the next few hours. A member of the ambulance crew who accompanied us tried to take his blood pressure but he was vehemently against it. As it was, they could not check to ensure that he wasn't physically unwell but it was clear to everyone that he was mentally unstable.

As the journey progressed, his eyes became wider and his mood alternated between troubled and anxious, and giggly and euphoric. He appeared to be smirking and then openly laughed at something or someone that we his fellow travellers could not see. He seemed far removed from these sad surroundings and was quite content to be living in this world of his own and after what seemed like an eternity, we reached the hospital. I have no idea how long it took us but it felt like a huge chunk out of my life.

IV

The building was a depressing sight; a 1960s ugly monstrosity that even animals shouldn't be housed in and was a most unwelcome sight for both patient and visitors. The ward we were escorted to was no better; dim, stark and unclean, you could see where patients, I presume, had been throwing things against the walls. They had obviously started off white but over the years had faded into brown and grey thanks to dust, dirt and, no doubt, shit that was hurled against them. And I'm sure you'd like to know about the smell, a smell that pervaded the air; well it was a mixture of old food, urine and the potent smell of bleach.

Sebastian walked ahead of me, unable to see my expression or the horror that I was witnessing. I'd never been on a general hospital ward let alone a psychiatric ward. I naturally didn't want to leave my brother here as I'm sure other relatives didn't want to either. An older gentleman, I presumed a patient, approached us. He was wearing dirty pyjamas, with stains of those lingering dinner smells, and smelt worse than Sebastian on a particularly bad day. A female nurse darted out of the nursing office and gently ushered him out of our way and back into what can loosely be described as the patient lounge.

Sebastian's demeanour had now changed and I could sense uneasiness in him, his steps became slower and he tried several times to stop walking altogether. He was also shivering due to the thin blanket that the ambulance service had provided. As we entered the office, I heard a high pitched scream, an agonising scream; like a bird, a crow which was being attacked by an animal. Within seconds three huge men ran down the corridor into the room nearest to the lounge and the sound ceased. The office door shut behind us, I felt safer but still scared. Sebastian was physically pushed on the shoulders down onto a chair by a nurse and the doctor who had accompanied us simply handed over some paperwork to the nurse and then left the ward. It was just me and Sebastian and Hazel, the ward manager. I began to pace with anxiety, my levels reaching the max. The office was small and there was nowhere to go apart from walking in small circles in the space designed for an upstanding light.

"What are we doing here? He said we would be talking about becoming one of God's angels. He lied to me; he didn't want to become an angel at all."

Thank God he was talking now; but spewing forth was delusion after delusion. I was so worried that he was going to remain silent through this whole experience that I was just so I was relieved he had said something. Hazel replied.

"You're in a hospital."

"To become an angel?"

I saw Hazel look at me and shake her head, clear that I shouldn't go along with his delusion, but I didn't know what to say in response. Thankfully she answered for me.

"You're in hospital because you're ill."

"You seem to be labouring under the wrong answer. I was tricked into coming here by this man here who claims, ridiculously I might add, to be my brother. We had an agreement and he has broken it. He is one who is ill, whoever he may be. He should be the one in here if he can't remember who he is. God won't make him an angel now."

"This hospital is for people with mental health issues, like we believe you have at the moment. Do you think you have issues such as these?"

"What a quaint way of putting it, mental health issues. Insanity, you can say it if you want. No man is insane there are only degrees of sanity. Is a man doing the same job for fifty years; with very little pay; who's only goal in life is to procreate, increase the world's overpopulation; buy a bigger house and spend his retirement growing vegetables, insane? Society dictates that this is normal. Tell me that's not insane. A man believes in a higher power transforming his very creation into angels is considered insane. Where did we all start from and where will most of us go? Think about that. It is a very logical and concrete answer to your question."

"So will you try and fly off a roof again if we allow you to just walk out of here?"

"Well I can't fly from a bottom floor window can I? They are probably waiting for me right now and I am here with, Hazel. I presume that's your name from your badge isn't it? And your friend here discussing my level of sanity. You are no different from me Hazel, remember that."

"Do you not think you should be here then Sebastian?"

"There's that name again. Why do you insist on calling me that, it's such a stupid pretentious name. You can call me Jesus. The Greeks however would pronounce the J as an H of course. You and your friend can Google it."

"I asked you whether you think you should be here."

"And I have answered enough."

Hazel backed off from the line of questioning and returned to the basics.

"You must be hungry. We'll get you some clothes."

"God will provide, Hazel; God will provide."

"Well until then, a nurse will take you to your room and help you get settled." She called over a rather large nurse, who looked like he belonged outside a nightclub as a bouncer.

"One final thing Sebastian, do you know what year and month it is?"

"It's the year of our Lord God."

The nurse, Evan, indicated to Seb to go with him, which he did compliantly. Hazel looked at me with an understanding 'I've done this many times before' look. I was coming apart and couldn't wait to get myself physically out of that dreary frightening place. I wanted out of this hell I was currently in. My brother had disappeared from reality and it scared the shit out of me.

"He needs to be sectioned Mr Bradbury, there is no way we can keep him as a voluntary patient. He will never agree to that as I'm sure you can appreciate. He's a danger to himself. I'll start the ball rolling for that to happen tonight."

"What if he tries to leave before then?"

"We do have powers to stop him from doing so which hopefully we won't have to use but I shouldn't worry at the moment; he's going nowhere."

"So sectioning, what does that entail exactly?"

"Two doctors and a social worker will assess him and then will either agree or disagree to the process. It will take a while for it to be organised. He would be placed under Section 2 which is an order for assessment and treatment. He will of course be medicated, possibly sedated, until we find a medication that works. A plan then will be made for his discharge. Section 2 is for up to 28 days but this is not concrete; it can either be less days or transferred over to a Section 3, which is for up to 6 months, but we'll cross that bridge if it arises. It needs to be done Mr Bradbury, he's a danger to himself at the moment and he cannot care for himself. Why don't you get yourself something to eat and some clothes for him and come back in a few of hours? We should have the outcome by then, but I think we all know what it is going to be."

I quickly excited the ward and once in the open air all the emotion a human being can muster erupted from the core of my very being. I pounded on the nearest wall; stamped my feet like a five year old; yelled every obscenity in the English language and finally succumbed to the exodus of every tear I'd ever held back. I cried like I've never cried before, glad that I was alone to express my utter devastation of what I was experiencing.

After what seemed like a few minutes I was able to compose myself sufficiently to order a taxi back into Cambridge and retrieve some clothes and other items for Sebastian. I failed to notice that my phone battery was close to zero. Nothing in his room was where you would expect it to be. Fresh clothes were still in his case, which was hidden away at the top of his wardrobe; he must have been living in the same clothes since he left home. His toothbrush was on the windowsill and there were two books under his pillow. The bed was completely stripped of any sheets and the mattress stained from what seemed like urine. Our parents would be appalled or disgusted; as for me I was unbearably sad and guilt ridden that it had come to this just weeks after he'd left the safety of our parents' house.

My father rang, when I had literally just closed the door, and I was in two minds as to whether to answer it; but I did.

"Dad"

"Well."

"He's in Hitherbrook Psychiatric Hospital. He's going to be sectioned, for up to 28 days. I've just picked some stuff for him. When are you coming up here?"

"Have you phoned your mother to tell her?"

"No. I'm waiting for you to. So when are you coming?"

"Probably at the weekend; if he's still there."

"Of course he's still going to be here. He's being sectioned; involuntary patient status. This is serious shit here, Dad. So you're not coming up here now? I'm trying to handle this all by myself and it is not working. I can't do it. He needs you Dad; he's frightened and I need you."

"He'll be taken care of Ben; it will blow over and we don't need to upset your mother. It's probably the best thing for him. Let me know how things pad out over the next few days."

"You're serious aren't you? You are going to let us deal with this by ourselves?"

"Don't be so dramatic Benjamin. You'll deal with it fine and he will be fine."

I tried to convince my father that the situation had gotten way out of control and that this was more than Sebastian just being admitted to hospital to have his tonsils out. It was typical of my father to be so blinkered on a subject that may require some sort of emotion. I knew that he would feel embarrassed by the situation and would rather it be swept under the £5,000 Persian rug that he was so fond of.

I passed a kebab shop on the way to the car but once in the car I couldn't eat it. I felt like vomiting so quickly opened the door in case I did. Once the urge passed I threw the kebab on the ground and tried to relax and remove the heavy anxiety that was weighing upon my shoulders and, mostly, the guilt I was feeling. Sebastian had been like this for months: the bizarre behaviour, the hiding, the things he said and the décor of his room. I had a sudden flashback of the wall covered in articles about apparitions and angels; and of course God. We, our parents and I, had watched from the side-lines Sebastian's descent into madness and had neither said nor done anything to prevent his uneasy mind gaining momentum and spiralling out of control.

I slumped back in the car allowing these thoughts to continue swimming in my brain. How could I have been so blind? My phone started to vibrate in my trouser pocket but I ignored it. I wasn't ready to talk to anyone just yet. After a few moments I took a few deep breaths and started the car for the journey back to the hospital. Like a bad omen it began to rain, like it had the first time that Father and I had had to go to Sebastian. As the hospital building came into view I was immediately depressed. Gone are the days when psychiatric hospitals were formed out of old Victorian asylums; which had their own grounds, gardens and workshops, were self-sufficient and were above all safe. I paid the car park fee which was an astonishing amount for a couple of hours.

With positive thinking and positive control I strode up to the ward. I hadn't noticed before but the ward name was Crocus, definitely not an indication of its pleasantry or beauty. Hazel met me at the door and briefed me with what was happening. The doctors were with him now and we should expect an outcome very soon. It was pretty clear what the outcome would be but the board has to satisfy themselves that the person needs to be admitted involuntarily, they would be crazy not to. Hazel told me of a case of a young man who was floridly delusional but managed to keep up an act of normality for at least an hour before he truly broke and revealed his true mind set of believing he lived in a television. It was a very bizarre case to inform me of but I got the picture nonetheless. She asked me to wait in the patient lounge.

There were two patients, I assumed, in the lounge both sitting incredibly close to the television set, ironically watching a hospital drama. They were absolutely captivated by it and the volume was turned up to the maximum so that I'm sure the people in Cambridge could probably hear it. Another patient ambled in and sat at a table close to the window. He didn't look like the others in appearance, whereas they wore dirty pyjamas and grotty dressing gowns, he wore a pair of unrumpled trousers and a shirt tucked in. Was he a patient? I wasn't sure.

It became apparent that he was when a few minutes later I saw him playing with a cutlery knife. Within seconds a male nurse was beside him and removed the knife from his grasp.

"How did you get the knife Robert? You know you're not allowed to have one. Go back to your room. Where is your nurse?"

Surely they must know where his nurse was. It was said as more of a command than a request to return to his room. The boy however, who must have been Sebastian's age, didn't pay any attention to the nurse and spontaneously erupted into tears in a somewhat childlike manner, yet agonisingly adult at the same time. A young girl, Melanie, who was a student nurse, went over to comfort him and relieve the nurse of this duty. She must have been the same age as him but unlike her fellow colleagues she provided a warmth and understanding to the situation but it was a good ten minutes before he showed any signs of calming down.

"Let's go back to your room. Your mum will be here soon."

I was captivated yet disturbed as to how this would play out. Melanie was now however seemingly out of her depth but persevered with great willing. Another nurse appeared carrying a small cup and a glass of water, Melanie stepped back allowing the other nurse to take over.

"Time for your medication. You must take it you know that. You won't get any better if you don't and I don't have time to stand around waiting for you."

She shoved the cup and glass at Melanie knowing she would be the good cop to her bad. "You try." Melanie crouched down beside him again offering the medication but even her gentle persuasion could not move him. He grabbed the two sides of the chair totally disengaged with what was going on, hoping to root himself to the chair. I continued watching guiltily curious to see the outcome. He looked unbelievably sad and, if I'm honest now, like a zombie. The other nurse returned, a nurse who reminded me of Nurse Ratchett in the film One Flew over the Cuckoo's Nest, to see how Melanie was progressing. Robert had stopped the anguish cries and was now snivelling and wiping his nose on the sleeve of his shirt.

"Your mother is on her way Robert. You don't want me to tell her that you are refusing your meds. She won't be happy if I tell her. You don't want that do you?"

I was a little dumbfounded. How do you make your patient feel better when you are threatening him to feel bad? It just didn't make an awful lot of sense to me. I bet he didn't give a flying fuck what his mother thought and felt at that moment. The medication wasn't going anywhere and neither was he. The situation didn't last much longer as no progress had been made. Melanie and Nurse Ratchett left him and I thought that was the end of it but it was far from it. As they left he looked in my direction and I just smiled uneasily at him.

What happened next, disturbed and affected me greatly as five nurses, three male and two females, all descended on him at once. Nurse Ratchett followed on behind flicking a syringe. Within ten seconds it was all over and poor Robert was off the chair onto the floor each nurse sitting on or pinning down a flailing limb as he writhed in protest. He was quickly injected and a heart-breaking scream left his mouth. His struggling ceased, he became calm and only then did the words be uttered from Nurse Ratchett's mouth, "You see what a good boy you can be." I deliberately looked at his face and he showed no emotion as his continued to be restrained. Did it really require five people to subdue a non-threatening teenager? After five minutes or so he was helped off the floor and assisted in walking back to his room. This would be a scene that would play out time again with Sebastian in the future months although his response would not be so placid.

Melanie stood in front of me, looking a little shell shocked from the experience, and asked me would I like a cup of tea. She led me into a small kitchen which had locks on everything. I studied her face which now looked a little upset.

"Are you okay?"

"Yeah, it's my first time on an acute ward. My other placements were in nursing homes and stuff."

"It's my first time on a ward too. Is it not what you expected?"

"Didn't know what to expect really. Nothing I think prepares you for it you know you see it on telly and everything. You're waiting for your brother Sebastian?"

"Yes. It's been quite a long time."

"I don't know how much longer. I'm not really involved in a lot of ward stuff."

"How long have you been here?"

"Only three weeks. I'm really enjoying it though. I've learnt a lot."

"You're doing a great job. I watched you with that young man."

"You mean Robert?"

"Yeah. He didn't look like a patient at first if you know what I mean?"

"I shouldn't be talking about other patients but he's my favourite. He's tried to kill himself loads of times. He's severely depressed. He's been here three weeks; he's on a Section 2. He needs a lot of attention; we've got to dress him and wash him and stuff. It's really sad. He's only 20. His mother comes every day to visit and he doesn't speak. When he first was admitted he spoke but it was very little; now he doesn't speak at all, barely opens his mouth even. Some days we have to even feed him but his mother does that if she's here. Can you imagine living like that and his mum is so nice too."

"What is going to happen to him?"

"They are thinking are doing ECT. Apparently it's really good for his type of illness. I've never seen it done though; don't know if I want to really."

"Isn't it something to do with electrical currents? I've seen it in the movies which I guess everyone has."

"I think it's to do with a fit or something. As I said I've never seen it but there was a young girl here a couple of weeks ago, who was on her eighth treatment, and she seemed fine to me afterwards and she said it worked."

"Eighth treatment?"

"Yeah, some people can have up to sixteen apparently."

I heard someone calling for Melanie so we quickly washed up the cups and put them away in the locked cupboard. I felt a little better talking with Melanie; even though she was a student she had flair with people and I hoped she would get along with Sebastian. A nurse I hadn't met before ushered me into the office and indicated for me to sit. I couldn't have cared less whether I sat, stood or performed circus tricks at this point in time. I'm sure she picked up my sense of irritation at the niceties before the bad news.

"Mr Bradbury, your brother has florid psychosis and he can no longer differentiate between fact and fiction. He's living in a world of complete fantasy and so he was sectioned for his own protection and that of others. It's a section 2 which I'm sure you've already been told is an assessment and treatment order. He can be here for up to 28 days depending on how successful the medication."

"Can he be transferred nearer London? Our parents live there. He's just a student here."

"Yes he can, but I wouldn't recommend it at the moment. He's seriously ill Mr Bradbury; it's best if he's settled and then you can make a decision after a few days."

"So what's his diagnosis then?"

"It's too early to say as there are many illnesses which have degrees of psychosis and it's not wise to label at the beginning. There are illnesses, such as depression or bipolar, which can exhibit such behaviour not just conditions such as schizophrenia which most people have heard about."

"Can we appeal if we want?"

"Sebastian can if he chooses to but this way, although to you it may be harsh, he can be medicated and monitored in a safe environment. He may not have jumped from his college roof but there was certainly the possibility of him falling off."

"Can I speak to his Doctor?"

"He will be allocated a doctor tomorrow and you can phone the ward for his progress. Ward rounds are on Fridays should you wish to speak to his doctor or raise any concerns."

"So this is it then? Can I see him now?"

"I'm sorry but that's not a good idea, as you can understand."

"Understand what? I want to see my brother."

"And I cannot allow it. Your presence may unsettle him so it's best to wait a couple of days. You can phone the ward everyday if you wish."

"Let me get things clear. You've locked up my brother, I cannot see his doctor and I cannot see him. Are you kidding me?"

"Far from it Mr Bradbury. This is the way things work. Your brother is safe, he's calm and he will be taken care of. It is out of your hands I'm afraid. You need to go home and get some sleep yourself and visit in a couple of days. Like I said, it's the best for him."

By now I was really pissed off. I had hit a brick wall and my nose was hurting like hell.

"I don't live a few miles away. I live in Sussex; our parents live in London. I cannot just walk out of here and return in a few days' time. I'm here, now."

"I understand your frustration, I really do," and it looked like she really did and I knew too that I was only one of many that she had had this conversation with, "however you must understand at this stage in his illness he may not recognise you or appreciate you and you may find that your time here at this stage is ill rewarded. So please, I know it's hard but just leave him a few days or wait until the weekend. Like I said you can phone the ward, twice a day if you wish, and we hopefully shall be able to tell you something positive."

She gently touched my arm and oddly it gave me a sense of security. I handed over Sebastian's bag of clothes, knowing full well he probably wouldn't wear them. As I said my thank you to her I felt the start of stinging in my eyes and that inability to swallow. As I made for a quick exit I noticed that a door was half open and a nurse was sitting, with her arms crossed, looking bored in the doorway. I walked slowly past and saw the curled up body of Robert on his bed and a woman, whom I presumed to be his mother, sitting beside him stroking his hair. As the door closed behind me I heard a desperate scream. I now was running, running hard until I reached the welcome sight of the car park. I was sure of one thing; I wasn't leaving my brother there.

I had nowhere to stay so drove back into Cambridge to find a bed and breakfast, but then hoped that Sebastian's room would still be unlocked so I would go and crash there for the night. I very much doubted that anyone would want to steal anything from his bizarre den. On the contrary it would probably be used as a dumping ground. I had no idea of the time and of course all of Sebastian's time instruments were either broken or covered with reams of masking tape. I made up a poor excuse for a bed and was just about to lie down when I felt a presence behind me.

"Mr Bradbury."

"Jesus! Ms Latimer. You nearly scared the shit out of me…"

"Sorry. It's been so chaotic we forgot to lock Sebastian's door. How is he?"

"Not good at all. Sorry I'm just all over the place. I'm probably not even coherent."

"Why don't you come back and stay at mine for the night. You can't stay here. You look like you need some food. I just live across the quad. It's no problem."

By now I was past caring that I had met this woman only once before and I was just about to stay with her for the night. A real bed or comfortable sofa seemed much more inviting than trying to sleep around the stains on a mattress. Her rooms were small but comfortable.

"It's very small and pokey, I know, but it suits my OCD tendencies. Please make yourself comfortable; are you warm enough? It can be like Siberia in here sometimes."

The sofa and its eight cushions were so soft I sank down into them feeling that they were going to swallow me up.

"Drink? Coffee?"

"Do you have anything stronger?"

"Whisky?"

"Thanks."

"Do you want something to eat? A sandwich or something? It's one of the only things food-wise I can make."

"No thanks. What time is it?"

"11.30"

"I never wear a watch as I don't need time schedules. I paint when the sun rises until the sun sets. I use the natural sundial."

"You're a painter, professional?

"Yeah, my main work is commissions and that allows me to paint what I love doing; landscapes." I was beginning to feel very drowsy and my eyes were beginning to close with every sentence that I uttered.

I was rather disorientated when I woke and attempted to take in my surroundings. The clock on the mantel piece said 6.30 so I just closed my eyes and was awakened what seemed like five minutes later with a smile and a cup of tea. I felt like I had a hangover and was waking up still in a mental stupor of what I did last night. She disappeared into the bathroom and I heard the shower running but the door wasn't quite closed. We didn't know each other, other than the ten minutes of conversation that we had had yesterday. Shamefully I could not remember her first name. I glanced around her sitting room hoping for clues; there were a few photos of her strategically placed but only one with her and a man. I presumed it must be her boyfriend and hoped to hell that he wouldn't walk through her door.

Everything was neat in place and the complete opposite of Sebastian's mess across the quad.

I propped myself up into sitting position; the jacket I was wearing yesterday was now placed at the foot of the sofa and my shoes on the floor beside me. I felt like shit and possibly looked like complete shit. It suddenly hit me. Susan, her name was Susan. I got off the sofa, folded the granny like knitted blanket and put on my shoes. Susan put her head around the door. She looked so different under these circumstances.

"Make yourself at home. I'll be with you in a second and make you some breakfast."

She came out the bathroom running her fingers through her wet hair and was tastefully covered by a large fluffy towel. She was much prettier than I had originally thought. I guessed she must have been in her mid to late thirties but looked a lot younger.

"I've left you a towel if you want a shower and there's a spare toothbrush on the windowsill. I told you I was very anal about things. Do you like scrambled egg? It's another one of my meagre culinary classics."

"This really is extraordinarily kind of you Ms..."

"Susan, just call me Susan."

"Okay Susan. Call me Ben; Benjamin only by my parents; and only when I'm in trouble."

"You get into trouble a lot do you Ben?"

Was she trying to flirt with me? I wasn't sure. It would be highly inappropriate given the circumstances but I was surprised it didn't bother me. To save myself any embarrassment I just smiled and quickly made for the bathroom shutting and locking the door behind me. The shower was the best feeling as I cleansed myself of the hospital smell from the day before. I just let the water cascade over my head as I stood there motionless with my eyes tightly closed. I felt a new sense of purpose and vigour. I had to remain in the clothes from yesterday but my skin felt more alive. When I exited the bathroom Susan was sitting on the sofa, a plate of scrambled eggs on her lap and holding out a plate for me.

"Thanks, that looks great. I'll have to get Cosmo from your friend; I really appreciate it as I know he is not exactly a Yorkshire terrier."

"Macie loves dogs; she's got three and they are all different breeds. She keeps trying to persuade me to get one but I'm not yet convinced. I'm a cat person. As a child we had a Siamese cat called Poodle because my sister really wanted a dog; so the poor cats name was a compromise. Poor thing must have been traumatised. I phoned Macie earlier and she's bringing Cosmo over. Oh and I've charged up your mobile phone. It fell out your pocket when you fell asleep and I noticed your battery was low."

"These eggs are really good; you do know how to cook."

"I've never really cooked breakfast before."

"Thanks again for everything. I just can't thank you enough."

"You seemed so alone in all this. Where are your parents?"

"At home; oblivious. Our father is a very old fashioned stoic man, he's a barrister and not one for scenes or hysteria or even emotion really. I think he's a very sad man covered over by bravado and doing the stiff upper lip thing that we're supposed to be so proud of. He cannot accept that Seb is not like others and never has been. I'm very close to my brother but it's not quite close enough. I'm four years older than him so we never really spent our teenage years together. My father expects him to be me. Apparently Seb is going to ride through it and come out a better man for it. It's just bloody ludicrous you know because nothing I say seems to make a difference. It always comes back to 'you are men just deal with it.' And our mother, she used to be happy; when I was a very small child she'd laugh and smile and she would shower us in hugs and affection but as we grew up our father's influence took its hold and she held both of us at arm's length. It affected my brother the most being the sensitive soul that he was, and is. We were left to fend for ourselves and make our way in the world without them. I think I coped but Sebastian, well I think we know what happened there. I'm sorry I didn't mean to talk at you with all this. I've never really spoken about our parents but to deprive Sebastian of them now just breaks my heart. You know there is a young boy on Sebastian's ward, severely depressed, doesn't talk, needs help with the basics of living and his mother visits every day and just sits beside him in silence. Here I am going on again. I'll get out your way as soon as I get Cosmo."

My head was bowed down as I said my speech mainly out of embarrassment but also out of shame that I could not have been there more often for Seb. Susan's dressing gown came unfolded at the leg slightly as she crossed her legs. She had nice legs, a bit skinner than Sophia's. I quickly averted my gaze.

"Are you going to visit him today?"

"They said not to. Apparently it is better for him and he may not recognise me anyway."

"I'm sorry that must be really upsetting but perhaps they may be right. You want him to be settled don't you and perhaps this is the only way to do it. You're going to be distraught if he doesn't recognise you or perhaps doesn't want you there, won't you?"

"Yes, I suppose so, but I've just let him down so much you know."

"How? You didn't make this happen. You didn't encourage him to get onto that roof. He did it because he is sick, Ben, not because of something you did or didn't do. It happened and it's being taken care of, he's lucky to have a brother like you."

I quickly wiped a tear from my cheek desperately trying to hide it. "We watched him as he grew more insular and bizarre and into someone who hid from the world, hid from us. We did nothing to stop it. He's been alone through all this and God I hate myself for it. He's in a filthy ward, probably now full of drugs and left alone in a room that looks like a prison cell. You cannot say anything to me that is going to make me feel remotely better about what we've done."

She put her plate down on the floor and wrapped an arm tightly around my shoulder holding me close. I wanted desperately to hold it together until I was alone but I couldn't do it. The emotions that I felt again just took over and I just effortlessly, pathetically sobbed on her shoulder. And it felt good, it felt so good to unburden the terrible feelings that I was experiencing with someone. She was my catharsis. I began to relax under her arm and began to feel much calmer. She said nothing; nor needed to say anything. It was perfect. It came to an end when her friend Macie arrived with Cosmo. I quickly nipped into the bathroom to wash my puffy red eyes and returned to greet her friend with a smile and gratitude. Cosmo barked when he saw me, so I knew at least someone loved me.

Macie was an odd woman. She looked in her 50s, perhaps even more; was only about 5ft tall and wore an array of dog whistles and remote devices around her neck, obviously tools to control her dogs. I offered her payment for looking after Cosmo but she politely refused saying he was a pleasure to look after. I wasn't convinced about that. I could hear dogs barking in the background and she was pulled away by their incessant noise.

"She seems, err, nice."

"Odd? Yeah she is that. She is my ex mother-in-law; long story. She still treats me like a daughter. My mother died when I married and she's kept in contact ever since. I'm very grateful to her she's been there a lot for me. I was only married for a couple of years; just one of life's mistakes."

She looked at the clock and this I took as an indication that it was time to go. She ran into her bedroom and appeared five minutes later in a flattering blouse and skirt and her hair tied back loosely in a ponytail. "Sorry if I've made you late."

"I'm not late; I'll be just on time. You can stay here longer if you wish, just pull the door when you go it locks automatically. I must go but if you, or Sebastian, need anything just let me know."

"You're a great cook, by the way."

"Yeah. One meal down; hundreds to go!"

"Thanks Susan."

"No problem."

With that she closed the door and was gone. I washed up my plate and laid it on the side and then grabbed my jacket. As I walked out to the car I felt somewhat rejuvenated. I was ready to tackle my parents, particularly my father, head on. This feeling naturally was short lived. The ward manager rang me to ask if I could come in and see Sebastian's doctor after lunch and if possible bring my parents with me. Thankfully the meeting would not take place on the ward. Of course I agreed and immediately rang my father. In a complete turnaround he agreed to drive up and would meet me for lunch beforehand.

After spending three hours of excruciating boredom wandering aimlessly around Cambridge, I chose a place to have lunch and just sat and waited for my father. My levels of anxiety were rapidly increasing and I didn't really know why at this stage; it was just my father not a firing squad. But he was a formidable force and I knew I had to get through to him the seriousness of Sebastian's illness and the consequences of what had happened over the last two days. He saw, I believed, mental illness to be a weakness of character and that only the meek and the mild succumb to it. When he eventually arrived the stern, everyday look on his face hadn't softened into concern or even compassion. We talked only of trivial matters such as the drive to Cambridge, the house boiler continuously breaking down and the arrangements for taking Cosmo back home. He was currently asleep in the car ensconced with half a packet of dog biscuits and a bowl, bought from Tesco's, and a bottle of mineral water. The dog was certainly living the high life. I was concerned about Sophia, as I had not spoken to her since the morning I left for Cambridge, and my phone mailbox was overflowing with unanswered messages. We talked of everything bar Sebastian. I was nervous about the meeting but I guess my father thought of it like a meeting at the Court and Sebastian and I were the defendants.

We waited in a pokey waiting room in what seemed like the basement of a derelict house. The plastic chairs had seen many arses on them and the magazines left out were circa 1980 when you could read of the wedding of Charles and Di and D list celebrities. There is nothing like living in a time warp and confusing your already confused patients. My father sat there; breathing very heavily through his nose; tapping his foot irritated. There were posters with the message 'Do you know someone with mental illness?' posted all around the waiting room. Would it not be obvious if they were sitting in a psychiatrist's waiting room? His secretary informed us that the doctor would be around half an hour late so my father made an audible sound of annoyance and left to get some fresh air. I smiled apologetically to the woman, who was only the messenger, as she huffed her way back into her little office no more than the size of the Harry Potter cupboard.

Father returned about 20 minutes later and resumed his seat a little calmer than when he left but proceeded to repeatedly look at his Rolex. The time ticked on and by now I too was getting ticked off. There was only so much you could read on celebrity sex lives. Forty minutes later the doctor appeared and what an appearance; he looked as though we should be reading him his last rites. His hair was so unruly he looked like he could have been related to Einstein. My heart sank, if appearances are anything to go by, and the look on my father's face spoke volumes.

"Mr Bradbury, I'm Dr Trimbull. Sorry I'm late; things always get behind. Please come in. And you are?"

"Ben, Sebastian's older brother."

"You were with him when they bought him in?"

The office was just as small as the secretary's cupboard. The walls, a dirty magnolia colour, were peeling and the office was full to the brim of patients' files and psychiatric text books. It was just as grim as the ward. He indicated for us to sit but it required him to move a vast quantity of papers so we both could sit down. My father spoke first.

"What is happening with regards to my son?"

"Sebastian has severe psychosis and for the moment he's heavily sedated. We need a clearer idea of what has been happening before this psychotic break so we can make an accurate diagnosis and treat him accordingly."

"What is his diagnosis?

"We can only make a preliminary diagnosis at this time. I understand he was trying to jump from a roof at his college." He was rifling through the crap on his desk, I assume, to try and find Sebastian's notes.

"He wasn't going to just jump off the roof. He told me that he was waiting for God to make him an angel and he would then be able to fly."

My father sat silent, unable to contribute anything.

"Any indication of unusual behaviour prior to yesterday? What about the few months or days before?"

"I don't live with my parents but to be honest he started to be quite bizarre this last year. He was studying for his A levels. He just shut himself away in his room. I don't live at home and can only comment on what I've seen sporadically; but he's been more than a little weird." My father looked at me in disbelief, ready to jump in.

"Ben, that is such an exaggeration; you were like him when you were studying. He worked diligently and got into a fine university. Any strangeness is just that adolescent phase of being miserable and uncooperative. He was never a happy child."

"Does he take any drugs, prescription or otherwise?"

"No, he does not."

Heaven forbid if Sebastian had smoked his first spliff. Even if he had done I doubt my father would ever admit to it. At least two months of my university days were spent in the haze of a marijuana induced fog. Unsurprisingly Dr Trimbull looked at me for the answer to that question so I just simply shook my head.

"What about relationship problems?"

"Is that entirely relevant?"

"All questions are relevant, Mr Bradbury. Relationship difficulties can cause stress; stress can lead to psychosis. You must try and understand that we know nothing about your son and he cannot provide us with the information. We try and treat patients holistically rather than just as an illness as it gives us more of an insight of his social environment and coping skills. We need to know whether he has tried to kill himself before, has he suffered bereavement, had depression or an eating disorder. The list you see goes on and on."

"I see."

I knew my father was stonewalling so I laid out my cards, "He hasn't tried to kill himself, not that I am aware of, but he is obsessed with death and suffering and religion. His room at home is full of magazines and books about miracles and disasters. He has a shocking picture of the crucifixion of Christ over his bed. You've never been in his room Dad and it is like a shrine in there. But the funny thing is that on the other wall are articles and pictures of the universe and stars and but also of alien encounters and abduction. It just doesn't correlate with the religion as its just poles apart in ideology. Books are in pristine condition and neatly ordered as if they had never been used or read. His room at college is different though; it's a mess and nothing is placed where you expect it to be. Books are under pillows; his toothbrush and toothpaste are outside on the windowsill; it looks like the room has been ransacked. You've probably smelt him too. I helped him dress the day he left for university and they are the same clothes he is wearing now. I doubt he's been efficient and washed them. He's like a tramp and he never used to be; used to take pride in his appearance. That disintegrated about a year ago. His bed also smells of urine, he seems to just lie on the mattress on the floor. It's just not him; this whole thing is just not him."

"You never told us this Ben."

"I tried to. On the morning he left with you for Cambridge I packed his clothes and books, I helped dress him and he then erupted into tears. You were just down stairs reading the paper, clock watching and reminiscing over your great university days."

"Benjamin, just stop."

"I can see that as a family you have many unresolved issues. This could have impacted on his mental state while changing to a new environment."

"Are you saying it is my wife and my fault he is in here?"

"Not at all; we don't assign blame. But you do need to be honest, certain behaviours fit into certain diagnostic criteria. We need to know what we are dealing with. People are often ashamed to say if their son or daughter has been violent or aggressive towards them or others or has had problems relating to sexual issues or hygiene. In mental health we deal with and try and cure something which we cannot visibly see. You can't take an x-ray and diagnose depression for instance. It's from the patient background and history that gives us the blueprint. If people want to assign blame then we leave that for the therapists to unravel."

"There's another thing I think you need to know. I went into Seb's room and I can't describe..... I found some of his journals in his desk, I know I invaded his privacy and stuff but I can't describe what I read fully because I didn't understand it. There were at least a hundred notebooks and I all of them were half encrypted. Those I did read were full of description of daylight dreams, nightmares and what seemed to be hallucinations. There was a reference to 'them' a lot but he never described it further. It was a disturbing read, there was just such a flight of ideas being put down on paper and most of them were pretty horrific. That's why I came to Cambridge yesterday; I read them and I wanted to see him. He didn't answer his phone and I was worried; not worried enough as it turns out."

"He managed to contain himself quite well last night with the sectioning board and they were very close to not enforcing it. He's obviously been functioning quite well with everything over the last few weeks. He appeared to be lucid and intelligent and had an explanation as to why he was on the roof but he fell at the final hurdle when he asked them if they were there for the ceremony of his becoming an angel and said that they were not dressed appropriately for the occasion. He was very calm about everything, calm before the storm I suspect as he has no idea why he is here."

"What do we do now?"

"Wait. We'll try medications available and see which one suits him; but I warn you that this doesn't happen overnight. He may try one or even three types of medication before we start to see an improvement and it's a rather long process I'm afraid. At the moment he's calm and compliant but as soon as he realises that door is locked permanently he may act quite differently. We're going to sedate him for the first few days and then start the anti-psychotics."

"Can he be moved near to me or my parents?"

"Yes there is that possibility; but do you really want to interrupt his treatment if you don't have to? They may want to try something different or have a very different approach. I would approach that wish with due care."

"My brother has schizophrenia hasn't he?"

"Like I said it's too early to label a patient; diagnosis is usually made after periods of illness not usually one episode. He could recover completely and never need medication for the rest of his life but we may have already labelled him with the schizophrenia diagnosis, which is a very complex illness to understand and an illness whose name is not given out lightly. The ramifications could be devastating, so at the moment we have diagnosed him as suffering from a psychotic episode without substance abuse."

"I've been told not to visit Sebastian for a few days: I want to see him; we all want to see him."

"It's not advisable at this early stage. He needs to be as calm as possible and family can provide stress, which we don't want. It's also not always a positive experience for the relative. It's a very fragile time at the beginning, you understand. Is there any history of mental illness in your family?"

There was a long pause before my father spoke out. "Well, my wife suffered post-natal depression after having Sebastian. It didn't last long maybe a few months."

My father had never spoken about this nor had my mother. He was very matter of fact about it, no emotion or a feeling of empathy was heard in his voice. It explained why he was reluctant to talk to my mother about Sebastian and I did wonder whether her depression in fact had lasted for many years.

"As I said, it's very early days and we should see an improvement over the next few weeks if not a little longer. Is there anything else that you would like me to clarify?"

As my father shook his head I asked the most basic question, "Will he fully recover from this?"

"I'm afraid, Mr Bradbury, I cannot say with any certainty. I'm sorry."

My father thanked him for his time and made a hasty exist out of the front door. I followed at the rear absorbing all that had been said. I felt I should have said much more but I didn't seem able to form the words in my head. I caught up with my father who was now on his phone. I thought he would be talking to Mum but as I stood beside him he was discussing a case with a colleague. I was incensed and not in full control of my mouth.

"Can you not put the phone down for just one bloody minute to talk to me about what's happening? Your son is fucking crazy and on a mental ward; doesn't that deserve some talk time?"

He slapped me; hard; straight across the side of my face. He then proceeded to get into the car without as much as a word. I got in the passenger side my face stinging and feeling like a chastised five year old. It stung for at least half an hour. He didn't speak until we were about half way home and even then it wasn't out of concern. Cosmo was getting irritated and I'm sure he needed a bathroom break. He began to bark.

"Shut that animal up."

I tried to calm Cosmo but he was paying no attention to me either.

"Can you not take that blasted dog to your home in Sussex?"

"Sophia doesn't like dogs, Dad; it would be very difficult to keep him there."

"Well we may just have to find another home for him."

The day was going from bad to worse. My brother is crazy, our dog is unwanted, my car is now stuck in Cambridge and a bigger surprise was waiting for me at my London home.

VI

I opened the door to find Sophia standing in the hallway with three suitcases. I presumed she had just arrived home. Everything would be okay, I'd tell Sophia everything and she'd make me feel at peace.

"You didn't phone me."

"I'm not staying; I'm leaving."

"You've been away for a couple of weeks; surely you're not going out there again."

"No. I'm leaving you Ben."

"Leaving me?"

"I've met someone else."

"What? Who? Why?"

"You know him I think. We met on a dig a few months ago."

"Were you even in Egypt?"

"Of course."

"How could you? How could you not tell me earlier? What could I have done for us? We've been together for four years and you're just going to walk out of here, with three suitcases and a few choice words. Can we sit and talk about this? I cannot get my head around this now: Sebastian is crazy and sectioned in a mental ward in Cambridge; our dog is going to be made homeless and my father is completely in denial that everything in our family is falling apart and I think I'm going crazy. So please, give me a break and stay. We can work things out; we always do. We make a good team. Please don't throw that away on a guy you met a few months ago. I thought we were stronger than that."

"I'm sorry; this has been on the cards for a while. You cannot deny that things have been very neutral between us both. We hardly see each other. You're so engrossed in your painting and I with my career that out paths are barely crossing. We can't live like this any longer. Think about it Ben, our periods away from each other don't strengthen our relationship; we are just growing further and further apart."

"What's his name?"

"It's not important."

"What's his name?"

"Elijah Montgomery."

"How pretentious."

"Oh Ben, don't be so childish. You've met him. He works in the antiquities department."

"Oh, that makes it all better does it?"

"I'm going now. We'll talk tomorrow about moving my things out. Again I'm really sorry about your brother; I know how much he means to you. Of course I'm really sorry about us. We've had some really good times; really good. But now I just feel stuck and want to move on. I must go Eli is waiting for me."

"Tell me, if I hadn't come home when I did when would you have told me? Would you have just left with no word? Or would you have continued the game? Strung me along for a few more months until it was convenient for you to end it?"

"I'm not like that Ben; you know that. I wanted to tell you before I left for Egypt but I didn't feel the time was right. I didn't know for sure what I wanted."

"When did you stop loving me Sophia?"

"I haven't"

She struggled to pick up her three suitcases but I'd have been a fool to help her walk out of our life together, so I watched from the window as her new lover took the cases from her and loaded the boot of the car. I retained my composure as he walked up the front few steps to retrieve the last suitcase. I stood and watched pathetically as my long term girlfriend, my best friend, drove away with the new love of her life. I wish I could have thumped him or confronted him but fighting was never a strong suit of mine; the embarrassment of my efforts would be worse than the hit. I just sat down on the sofa we chose together and wondered could this day get any shittier.

I woke up the next morning, still on the sofa, and still in my clothes and a whisky bottle was lying beside me. Luckily it had been only half full but it didn't stop the horrendous hangover that I woke up with. I was hoping that all of yesterday was a dream and I'd see Sophia at breakfast and would speak to Sebastian, who was still ensconced in his Cambridge rooms, but now everything had changed. Anyone who has been unceremoniously dumped can tell you how it feels although I couldn't feel any anger towards her or to him. We were, as she rightly said, living two separate lives; people who came together for a couple of months and then parted again. We spent more time alone than we did with each other. I wasn't prepared for this, not prepared at all. So it took a long time before the intense feelings dissipated and, if I'm totally honest, once over that initial shock the feeling of missing her never really left me.

She and her new beau Elijah came to pick up her stuff the same afternoon. She didn't want any of the furniture or other sundry items that we had purchased together. I got to keep the wok and a set of carving knives which we bought the day we moved into our London home she just collected her personal items and vast wardrobe of clothes and shoes. Elijah waited in his car, a brand new Mercedes, which was a palace compared to my 2006 VW Beetle. I thought he'd drive something flash. I felt quite numb though as she practically skipped happily out the door down to her new lover. I couldn't use the 'she's Italian' excuse anymore for her feisty behaviour. She actually loved another man and I couldn't accept it. I watched them drive away and I unenthusiastically made my way to bed to clear my head and recover from the previous night. I stopped by my studio before I retired and mournfully looked at the portrait I was yet to finish. It was Sophia lounging on our chaise lounge accompanied by Socrates and Sophocles. She looked radiant and so breathtakingly beautiful. I grabbed a pair of scissors of the desk and was just about to make an incision when I stopped short, put the scissors down and just carefully removed the portrait from my easel and placed it behind the other paintings

VII

I rang the ward first thing in the morning; it was now three days of staying away and ringing the ward for updates. Each time I was told that he was settled but that there was no real improvement in his condition. He was still heavily sedated and would be for the next few days. I arranged to visit that Saturday and hopefully would be accompanied by our father. I hadn't spoken to him since the last visit and due to the fact that my car was still parked in an alley in Cambridge I was relying on him for a lift there. I wasn't sure of how much he had told our mother and whether she would be able to visit or be allowed to visit. I hadn't told anyone about the breakup with Sophia as I was trying to save face from being dumped. The flat was now minimal, gone were the feminine items that had made it our home and gone were our two cats. I had never really liked them but they were part of our home.

I received a call that afternoon from my father who confirmed his visit with me to Sebastian. I was to meet him at their house and we would travel on to Cambridge. I then could retrieve my car and no doubt countless parking tickets. He told me that my mother wished to go but that she didn't wish to travel that far and find him asleep for the visit. I couldn't really gauge what her feelings were but it seemed there was certainly no urgency about her seeing her son and my father was so indifferent to the situation that they seemed almost ashamed or embarrassed about it. Both my parents due to their upbringing had also never set foot on an NHS ward which signalled a somewhat superior attitude. It seemed like they felt that this incident had downgraded them to the status of the common man. I was somewhat surprised that my father hadn't mentioned a private hospital in our meeting with Dr Trimbull although I'm sure it was on the cards.

I spent the next couple of days in solitary confinement, painting and sketching until all hours, eating takeaway pizza and generally acting like a slob. The day before we were due to visit, I received a phone call from the ward manager stating that Sebastian had had a good day and that very slowly he should improve. He still of course was still terribly unwell and the psychosis hadn't receded but it was positive news. After hearing that I began to feel a little rejuvenated and started to clean up the house and put myself in order. For some inexplicable reason I later shaved off the beard. I think perhaps it indicated a new start for me without Sophia and while I wasn't intentionally looking for new love and company it was a way to feel free to do so.

By the time Saturday arrived I felt like a new man who was ready to face the world. My father of course was waiting impatiently for me, unaware of the unreliability of public transport. It was nice however to sink into the comfortable seat in the Bentley. Cosmo would never experience the Bentley again after the last time and I'm sure my father had the car valeted afterwards. Cosmo was housed in a kennel, albeit a large kennel, outside the house. He wasn't allowed on the lawn or in the house so he was surprisingly well behaved dog considering his circumstances. I had made the decision also to sell the London house and remain in Sussex, taking Cosmo with me. This would take place however after Sebastian's first admission.

The journey to Cambridge was non eventful. I told him of the split from Sophia and my decision to sell the house. I was never sure whether my parents particularly liked Sophia. She was very gregarious perhaps a little flirty, perhaps too flirty for their liking, and wasn't afraid to speak her mind. My father and she often got into heated discussions which of course he believed to have won. My mother was somewhat indifferent towards her. She felt she wore too much make-up and clothing that bordered on provocative but never said anything particularly challenging about her. I always thought my parents would have preferred me to have had dates with girls that wore knee length skirts, had a job as a lawyer and played the cello. I wanted more excitement from the humdrum existence of the family cocoon and Sophia provided that.

I never bought up the slapping incident; I just let it slide because my father was a man who could not be moved. I knew he wasn't capable of strong emotions and I think he expected that his children would also be. Children always see their parents through rose coloured spectacles and only realise when they grow up that they are flawed human beings. Babies do not come with a manual of practical parenting but some parents, sadly like Sebastian's and mine, didn't even read an instruction card. I had to be there for Sebastian if he was ever going to have a full and successful life.

By the time we arrived in Cambridge, that new zest for life I had been feeling that morning had departed and I started to feel depressed, even more so as we pulled up at the hospital.

"What in the name is this god awful place Ben?"

"It's Hitherbrook."

"Whatever it is, it's appalling, appalling that my son is in there."

"He doesn't really know where he is but I agree it's just awful. Can we forgo the niceties and just go and see him?"

We were buzzed onto the ward, I saw my father tense his body and start to breathe very heavily through his nose. He also looked like he wanted to avoid touching anything, as if he'd get some communicable disease. Hazel met us briefly said how he'd been and that she would speak to us both later after we'd seen him. My father requested that initially he'd just like to stay in the office and allow me to see him first.

Sitting in the entrance door of his room sat a very large black male nurse, his arms were folded and his attention was intently focused in the room. I tentatively approached. The nurse just waved me in. There Sebastian sat cross legged on his mattress which was stripped bare and on the floor. The bed frame was pushed up against the window blocking out any natural light. He was dressed in pyjama bottoms which too short in the leg, he was still sporting the beard and his hair was still unwashed and long. I tentatively stepped across the threshold into his room. He spoke first.

"Oh look, it's the guy who thinks he's my brother."

The nurse shook his head. "He is your brother."

"So he claims. So what can I do for you my brother?"

"I've come to visit you."

"And why is that important to you Ben? That's your name isn't it?"

"Because I want to see you; that you are being looked after."

"Well its five star accommodation here Ben, you should check in. Food's not bad but they are no Michelin chefs. Oh and this kind gentleman goes with me everywhere. I can't even take a piss without it being recorded for You Tube."

"Did you get the clothes I left for you?"

"They sure ain't Saville Row."

I motioned to a plastic chair, dirty of course, which countless of behinds had sat on. "Can I sit?"

"I don't know. Can you?" He looked at the nurse, Errol, with a wry smile across his face. Errol did not return the smile. He looked so much like a bouncer in a nightclub who utters the words 'If your names not down you're not coming in' every Friday and Saturday night.

"Behave Sebastian."

"He's such a party pooper is Errol. So Benjamin, what do you want to talk about? As you can see I'm not going anywhere."

"Dad's outside, he'd like to see you."

"Why are you all claiming to be my relatives? God is my only father and as I'm aware he's not sitting outside."

"Do you need me to bring you anything? Some of your books?"

"I don't need books, I soak in information like osmosis and they are just books which are captors of energy. All of life's energy is held within the books' pages and are waiting to be opened and released into the atmosphere, which is then absorbed by me. Everyone in the world is providing me with intellectual stimulation and, of course, Errol here is such scintillating conversation; he keeps me amused for hours. Oh look Benjamin, here comes Lilly with my smarties. Don't you think her very pretty?"

"Um, well......"

"That's okay; you don't need to answer if you don't wish to."

An extremely pretty nurse, as Sebastian had suggested, was standing in the doorway with a glass of water and a small pot which I assumed contained his medication.

"Okay, Sebastian you know the drill."

He was required to get up of the floor and stand in front of her while she emptied the pot of pills into the palm of his hand. He readily took them, which I was quite surprised at, opened his mouth for her to check that he wasn't concealing them and then returned to his monk like position on the floor.

"Why thank you Lilly, it's always a pleasure,"

"Behave, I'm watching you."

"And I you."

This person wasn't my brother as my brother was shy and gentle. What was this illness that had made him into the person who was in front of me? It sickened me and I didn't want to stay with him like this. "Well I must go now. It was so nice to see you." I don't know if I had done or said something wrong but as I turned to leave, he leapt of the floor so quickly I could barely notice it and then lunged at me. He was just inches away from my neck when Errol's huge arm prevented him from making contact and seconds later had him pinned down on the floor, face down on the mattress.

"Get the fuck off me."

"Not until you calm down."

"Fuck you; you bastard."

"You are going to get an injection if you don't stop struggling and sit up like a good boy and play nice. Say goodbye to your brother."

Three other nurses has arrived by now and had him restrained on the floor. I just quietly slipped out the door and went to find my father. Sebastian was still swearing like a sailor. Hazel caught us as we were making our way to the door.

"Mr Bradbury, can I have a word with you both. Please can we talk in the office?"

I really wanted to leave and my father looked disturbed and uncomfortable. "Why doesn't he recognise me? He nearly attacked me."

"Sebastian lives in a world that he perceives as threatening, you are part of that. Paranoia is a key component of psychosis. He lives in fear and fact and fiction have become indistinguishable and you are now one of those fears. You must understand these are very early days. We do not expect to see a considerable remission just yet. He still needs sedating. He's going to be here quite a while yet. He's tried to climb out a small window in the bathroom last night and has made several attempts to run to the door. As you see he has one-to-one nursing at all times."

My father stood rooted to the spot completely out of his comfort zone and when he spoke it was forthright and without emotion. He had his court persona on, "What are you doing about that?"

"All that we can. He's medicated of course and supervised but we just have to wait for the medication to take full effect I'm afraid."

"Is there nothing you can do to speed up this process?"

"No I'm afraid not."

I plucked up the courage to ask the question that had been on my mind for a few days now, "He has schizophrenia hasn't he? You know he has. I've been reading up about it and he seems to fit, the situation seems to fit."

"I'm sorry, we have been told no definite diagnosis as yet. Look, he's being treated for psychosis like every other patient. His doctor will tell you more, I'm sorry I can't be more definitive."

"Why did he try and attack me?"

"He perceives anything outside his fantasy as a threat and you are, as we all are, a part of that threat. I would suggest that you leave it a week or so before you visit again. Go home and look after yourself. We'll take care of him."

My father nodded a note of thanks and strode towards the door. There was something I needed to know. I had heard two nurses talking as we came through the door. "I overheard that one of your patients committed suicide on the ward how can I be sure that Sebastian won't do the same?"

"Robert was severely depressed and had been for a long time. He tried many times before to kill himself, even with close supervision. It can and does happen but I don't believe Sebastian would do that as he is waiting for something amazing to happen and I believe he'll carry on waiting. They are two very different people with very different illnesses. He's being taken care of Mr Bradbury."

"Thanks."

"Ring the ward if you have any concerns."

"Thanks again."

I walked to the door replaying Sebastian's attempt to attack me. Hazel made some impression with her explanation but I was desperately trying to understand it in my own messed up brain. On my way out the door I bumped into Melanie.

"Hey I heard what happened to Robert. How did it happen?"

"His mum left her scarf in his room while visiting him. Somehow he managed to hide it and then a nurse was doing checks during the night, he found him strangled. He'd tied himself to the door handle. They tried to revive him and everything but they couldn't. It was just awful here, really awful. His mother must be distraught you know, knowing that she had left the scarf behind. He wasn't getting any better and I suppose he just couldn't take anymore. The atmosphere around here is really weird and nurses are checking every patients every ten minutes and are like hyper vigilant."

"I thought it would be impossible for that to happen?"

"I know, everyone is being interviewed and stuff."

"Are you okay?"

"Oh yeah. It was a bit of a shock and everything but I suppose I'll have to get used to dealing with situations like this. His funeral is on Wednesday and a few of the nurses are going."

"What about you?"

"I don't know, I've never been to a funeral before, I'm a little scared to be honest. I don't know what of, dying I suppose, but I'd like to be there for him, you know. I got on so well with him, it's kind of upsetting to think that I was with him only a couple of hours before. But Sebastian seems quite sweet, I don't have much to do with him through but he seems quite safe to be with. I'm not allowed to be with some patients at the moment so I can't be with Sebastian."

"It's nice to see you again; you'll make a really good nurse Melanie."

"Thanks."

She skipped off in the direction of the noisy patients lounge. My father was waiting in the car, in the passenger side he could only be described as shell shocked. He was staring straight ahead, motionless. The keys were in the ignition and the car was running, "Dad, are you okay?" There was no reply. "Do you want me to drive home?" I was quietly hoping the answer would be yes as I was dying to get behind the wheel of his Bentley again. I probably wasn't insured and that would be a problem for a barrister. "I'll go get us drink, I think we both need it." I turned off the engine and walked back to the drinks machine in the hospital lobby. There was only coca cola and, for the first time ever, I saw my father drink cola and out of a can.

"What was he like Benjamin?"

"Not good, not good at all. He didn't recognize me, as me or as his brother."

"I told your mother he was in hospital with pneumonia, you will do the same."

"Why? You said Mum had post natal depression. You or Mum has never bought it up before."

"She had psychosis after giving birth to Sebastian. Your mother was in hospital for a month after she almost drowned him in the bath. We've managed to keep it quiet for many years and it is certainly not something we wanted to tell you or Sebastian. It was a dreadfully difficult time for both of us but I watched your mother be taken from me. I do know Benjamin what a psychiatric ward is like and I know it's not pleasant or an environment in which you wish anyone to be in."

"But Sebastian is in that environment right now."

"I can't deal with that at the moment."

"Jesus he is a kid, your protecting your own selfish needs rather than the needs of your own son, your own child. How exactly does that work? Pretend he doesn't exist and carry on? Do you think distancing yourself from him is going to make it easier, for Sebastian, for you, Mum or me?"

"Yes, I suppose I do."

"You suppose so. Right, just excellent. Well it doesn't work like that. You know more about this than me and I'm fumbling my arse off in the dark here. You sit here and basically turn your back on your sons. And you know what Dad, he attacked me; Sebastian attacked me and I ain't going anywhere. You know what, I just feel sorry for you. I'll get a bus into town." I charged out the door slamming it closed. I very rarely get angry but then I was like a bull in a china shop. I was muttering 'bastard what a total bastard,' to myself like I was, yes, a crazy person. I thought he would follow me in the car or catch up on foot but I looked back and he was gone. It was déjà vu standing at that bus stop and I did what all British people do, I stood in the queue and made eye contact with no-one.

I heard a familiar voice calling when I got off the bus in town. It was Susan.

"Hi Ben. How are you? Have you been to visit Sebastian?"

"Yeah, I have."

"I've just been doing a bit of shopping. Didn't go well?"

"No. You can say that ten times over and it wouldn't be enough."

"I'm so sorry. How about we go and get a coffee and you can tell me all about it? It may help."

"That would be nice."

Susan led me to a small café situated in one of the back streets of town. It was quiet and most welcome after the pullulating tourists in the streets. I had no appetite but ordered a sandwich to compensate for the energy I had released when I left my father seething with hate. In no time I was pouring out the experience of the visit and the selfish behaviour of my father. And I was surprised at her reaction.

"It seems to me like he is struggling with this just as much as you are Ben, especially if your mother was ill. I'm not saying that he's right but it's got to touch a nerve when another member of the family becomes ill. Don't you think it's only natural that he's going to shy away from and hold it at a distance? It must be bringing up some dreadful memories. He's hurting Ben, just as much as you are. I think you need to give him time to absorb it all and then of course accept it."

"My mother nearly drowned Sebastian in the bath when he was only weeks old."

"Oh my God. How? Why?"

"My father wouldn't go into details but that is why she was put in hospital."

"That is just awful; to watch your wife and then your son go through mental illness must be hell. You're going to have to be strong for him too."

"He's a soulless man Susan."

"That's not true."

"He's not suffering for Sebastian; he is suffering for himself. He deals in facts and there is just so much uncertainty that he completely won't accept anything else. It's like he's trying to hide a completely different life with my mother."

"I know I don't know him but...."

"I don't even know him."

"I'd give him a chance to prove that he can deal with Sebastian."

"I'm not convinced."

"Tell me. How is Sebastian? You seem reluctant to say. Do you want to tell me? Oh God I sound like a therapist."

"He tried to attack, nearly strangled, me. His nurse who is the size of nightclub bouncer managed to hold him just before he touched me."

She listened intently, continuing eye contact and making all the right noises. She was incredibly easy to talk to. Every now and then she would lean forward and place her hand over mine. She had a gentleness about her that lowered my anxiety levels and I felt a compulsion to continue talking.

"I'm sorry to hear that."

"There is no need to be sorry. He didn't even recognise me. He was obsessed with God and still believes he's the saviour of the people. You know I was actually scared of him. I was scared shitless of my own brother. I was with him five minutes, if that, and it ended abruptly with him lunging at me. I don't know if I can deal with this as I feel I'm on a rollercoaster in my own little Alton Towers which never ends, sometimes calm and then, wham, I'm falling 500ft. After I left my father, my rage and my fear subsided on the bus because a young child, seated with his mother in front of me, was describing everything that the bus had passed. His mother naturally began to get bored so he turned around to me and enthusiastically told me instead. It was bizarre but for that moment I felt happy. I had hoped that Sophia and I would have had children and it gave me a sense of hope. Does that seem strange to you?"

"Nothing about that is strange; children bring out the best of people by their total innocence of the world."

"He looks nothing like my little brother anymore; he just looks like a tramp. I don't know whether they can make him wash and put on clean clothes but I'd wish they try."

"Why don't you try and talk to your mum."

"I couldn't"

"Why not? She may be willing and comfortable telling you. She'll want to help her own son."

"No, she's like him both are emotionally shut down from Seb and I."

"She might surprise you."

"Well I'm not going to find out."

"Before you fell asleep on your last visit you were telling me about your painting."

"Well I got my first paint set at age four, spoilt the front room carpet with poster paint then voila I was painting for a living. I'm extremely lucky, I know, to have a profession which I love, not many people have the good fortune to do so. Sebastian loves drawing too it's something that bonds us a brothers. We can sit for hours painting or studying art books. I'd like to take him to Italy as he loves Italian art. I have to do tedious portraits every now and then with po-faced families but it pays for the rest of my work. What about you? Do you love your job or is it a means to do something else?"

"Oh I love my job too; I have been here almost five years now. I love Cambridge as a town. I've been very happy here. I'm from Newton Abbott so you can imagine the exciting life I must have led. It wasn't too bad but I was glad to get away to university especially after my father died, he had a heart attack. It wasn't the same though; families are never the same after someone dies. Does your girlfriend paint?"

"No, I'm new to single life again after four years."

"I'm sorry for asking, I didn't want to pry or put you in an awkward position."

"She found someone else; a colleague of hers; some bloke with a poncy name. I don't think I've taken it in fully yet. Her stuffs gone but she still resonates in the house, which I'm going to sell now. What about you? Do you have a man hidden under your bed?"

"I was married; I think I told you, for a brief time. I don't know if it was the physical thing or emotional part but Tom was a good part of my life even for the short while we were married."

"What happened?"

"Tom turned out to be gay. He was like many a homosexual man living the life of a heterosexual man."

"Didn't you get, you know, a vibe or something?"

"You'd think so wouldn't you as we'd been dating and then married for a couple of years? I guess I was too blinded by love. He was so perfect but for another man."

"When did, how did he tell you, or did he tell you?"

"We had a party at our house, all his friends were single males and he just looked far more comfortable in their company than he ever did with me and my friends. I confronted Tom about it and he told me straight out that he was gay and that he couldn't continue to live a life of someone that he wasn't. You know I went through that same questioning of whether I had turned him gay. He was my prince charming. We are still in contact; he's in a relationship with an actor called Peter for the last five or so years. They are so totally in love that I'm quite envious, not of Peter being with Tom but of their total commitment to each other."

There was a real sadness in her voice as she relayed her story. It was obvious to me that she truly loved the guy and still did but I felt impotent in replying as I had no experience of her situation and I confess that I had no knowledge of any of my friends being gay. I thought that that was the time to call it a day before we laboured on past relationships and poor relationship judgements.

"Well, it's been great talking with you but I think I need to get going soon. Do you want another coffee before I leave?"

"If you don't mind staying a little bit longer. You probably think I am an old spinster, living in a badly decorated house with ten cats."

"God I hate cats. Sorry."

Although Susan was more than ten years older than me, I felt her very much my contemporary in thought and action. I felt so at ease in her presence that it was as if I had known her for years. A wisp of hair kept falling in front of her eye and I was so tempted to gently brush it away.

"So will you drive to Sussex from here?"

"Yeah, I'm going to avoid my parents for now. I can't visit Seb for a week so I'm going to wallow in my own misery until then". We talked on for a least another hour before I made the definitive decision to leave. My mind and my body said I didn't want to. We eventually found my car, ticketed and clamped. Susan gave out a small nervous laugh and threw her hand to her mouth in embarrassment. What could I do but laugh too.

"Shit. Shitty; shit; shit."

"That's a lot of shit Ben."

"Sebastian's God is certainly trying my patience. Could today get any worse? Tell me is it Groundhog Day?"

Susan handed me the ticket for the clamping company. I was ready to head for home an hour or so later. We stood near my car that awkward feeling, particularly the male species arose: do I kiss her goodbye, or just shake her hand, perhaps slap her playfully on the back. I made the decision and leant in for a very quick kiss on the cheek which seemed to be appropriate. We parted company and yes I did grin broadly all the journey home. I was planning my next trip to Cambridge before I'd even left. All thought of Sebastian had dissipated in that trip home and my brain was thankful for a break. My last thought of Susan before I fell asleep that night was the image of her in her low cut dressing gown, showing the outline of her cleavage and her long smooth legs as she sat beside me in her flat. I wouldn't need excuses to see her again.

VIII

I woke up violently that night from a nightmare, drenched in sweat and panting so hard it was as if I was a Labrador. I fumbled for the light switch, my hands shaking. My sheets were sticking to my skin with the sweat. It took a few minutes to truly calm down. When I had recovered I opened the window and lapped up the cool breeze.

I remember the dream vividly. I was climbing some steep stairs, stairs that never seemed to end. I was dressed in mourning clothes and was carrying a large bible. A figure of a woman begins to descend the stairs towards me; she smiles, her arms are behind her back. We never meet; it is as if we are on opposing escalators. The woman brings her hands to the front and they contain a parcel. She violently throws the parcel at my feet. The paper unravels to reveal a baby; the baby has no face.

The dream disturbed me enough to telephone my mother and arrange a visit when my father was at work. I continued to phone the ward to check on Sebastian but the answer was always the same: "No change." I had resisted the urge to phone Susan but, of course, I hoped she was doing the same for me. My mind was too disrupted to concentrate on any work related painting so I spent a lot of time sketching outside; even under a huge umbrella when it rained. I contemplated my situation and tried to make sense of it. Sebastian was the quiet studious boy with great potential; I was the fuck up of the family and as I, a successful painter, looked at the beauty in front of me as he sat in his own stench on the floor in a filthy room in a NHS hospital for crazies.

I drove up to my parents', against my better judgement, to talk to my mother about her experiences. It would however be on the pretext of taking Cosmo off their hands to live with me, which I knew she'd be glad of. Questions were tumbling in my head like it was a washing machine. I had no idea how I was going to broach the subject; it's not the sort of question that arises while tucking in to tea and scones. I drove past the house a couple of times before I drove up the driveway. For some inexplicable reason my legs began to shake. What on earth was I afraid of? She was just my mother.

We spent frivolous time talking of the garden, the boiler, which kept breaking down, and the 'noisy neighbours' who were aged 81 and 76 which seemed highly unlikely. I used to wonder whether they had died on more than one occasion. She mentioned Sebastian first.

"How is he? Has he gotten over the worst yet? It's probably all those nasty germs in his room."

"Mum, what has Dad told you about Sebastian?"

"Your father said he's got pneumonia. He's got dreadful hygiene."

"Mum."

"Yes dear."

"Sebastian hasn't got pneumonia. Here's got severe psychosis, he's in a psychiatric hospital. Dad is lying to you."

"Why would he do that?"

"To protect you."

"Protect me; from what?"

"I know what happened with Sebastian; when he was born; your psychosis. Dad told me and he asked me not to ask you but..."

"You thought you'd hurt me anyway."

"It's not like that, at all; I just want to know what is best for Sebastian and as you'd experienced something like it I thought."

"You thought wrong."

"I'm sorry; I just want to know what it is like and how you managed to get through it. He's frightened, I'm frightened. You are supposed to be the one who tells us it will all be okay. I'm dealing with this alone and I don't know that I'm doing what is right. You're his mother, for God's sake stand up to the plate and be his mother. We are supposed to be his family." I know I was risking another slap across the face but I couldn't stand by and let my mother abandon him. She remained stoic and unmoved by my impassioned plea and simply poured herself another cup of tea as if I was just talking about the weather. I grabbed my coat and headed out the door incensed. "By the way I'm taking the dog."

My mobile rang as I had just loaded Cosmo and his possessions in the car. He was terribly excited; I don't blame him I'd saved him from a fate worse than death in that house. Sebastian's doctor needed to see us and we arranged to meet the next Monday. I would phone my father when I got home to tell him. I set off for Sussex, still somewhat enraged but capable of driving carefully. I threw a George Michael CD in the console and let his emotional problems wash over me instead. I always tried to believe that there were people with worse problems than my own and that I should be grateful. Now I thought it was total bullshit. Cosmo sat in the passenger seat beside me with his head out the half open window without a care in the world. I wish we could have exchanged places.

The drive back was interrupted by road works and traffic jams but it gave my brain a chance to organise my thoughts more clearly and try to comprehend my mother's response. I thought I remembered a happy woman when Sebastian and I were children but with hindsight she was a stand offish type of woman even with us. She kept her emotions very much to herself, she never mixed with our friends' parents or the other mothers at school. Whereas my friends' parents were very giving of their time and indicated to their children that they were indeed their most cherished possession Sebastian and I were treated as mini adults.

You would have thought that Sebastian, being the youngest in the family, would be far more indulged but that never happened. We were left to our own devices most of the time while our parents continued to socialise with their chosen set of privileged people. These were mostly my father's friends to which my mother had to feign enthusiasm or interest. They were two selfish people who lived a very selfish life. My father's work would come before anything else. I cannot recall him ever watching a rugger or cricket match when we were at school. He cared more and received more pleasure from the criminals he prosecuted. Perhaps Seb and I would have been better off if we had murdered someone.

Looking back it was Sebastian that always received the rough end of the stick from my mother. She treated him when he was a very small child like he had some contagious disease. I remember her hugging him and trying to be affectionate but discreetly kept him at arm's length. I remember one time we went to feed the ducks at Barnes pond when we were about 8 and 4 years old, we were each given a bag of breadcrumbs to take with us. Sebastian's bag had developed a hole and the breadcrumbs fell through before we reached the pond. Rather than dividing mine, she just sat him on a park bench and accompanied me to the edge of the pond. Sebastian naturally began to cry but was immediately chastised for being silly over such a small thing. He continued to cry until we reached home but was not once comforted or given something else to make up for it. There was an odd ness to her behaviour towards him that I clearly recognise now and I don't know whether she hated him or just had immense regret that she got pregnant with him.

So as you see, we never had an 'innocent' childhood but we were always guilty of something; even of just being born. I'm stronger emotionally than Sebastian but our father expected no weakness but for us to 'act like a man.' We had to put away the childish things and become miniature versions of him. I managed to stay the course, just, but Sebastian began to flounder when he reached his teenage years. A sensitive soul had developed and my guess is that they became ashamed of him. Even the poor dog was treated with distain.

Cosmo, thankfully, was overwhelmed at his new environment. He was a little hesitant when I opened the front door and encouraged him to walk in. He had lived his life in a garden kennel in all weather. He was of course fed and watered but he had very little freedom. It didn't take too long for him to find his feet. I saw the answerphone flashing. I'd become nervous of the phone now, living in fear of bad news about Seb. I organised myself and settled back in before I pressed play. It was one of those damn cold callers who don't leave a message but spend long enough on your phone for the message button to beep. I did however receive a letter from Sophia. My heart missed a beat as

I opened it hoping that she had reconsidered our relationship.

The letter contained no such thing; it started with the pleasantries and got down quite quickly as to why she was writing. Apparently while she was in Egypt she had tried to get a hold of me, she couldn't so she rang my parents' number. Very surprisingly Sebastian answered the phone; she too was taken aback by this but spoke to him for a few minutes. She said that he didn't make much sense but he made reference to being under surveillance although he didn't clarify by whom. She went onto say that he had said that he had removed all traces of any bugging devices and had hidden them in his special place in his room and that he was utterly convinced about this. Due to our break-up circumstances she forgot to mention it but once remembered she couldn't forget as he sounded so genuine. God only knows where his special place was, even if it existed and it was probably nothing but I rang my father about the meeting with his doctor and could he look around Sebastian's room, for what, I had no idea. He was reticent and said that he may not have the time and could I, whom he assumed had copious amounts of free time, come up and do it. I couldn't not; so again I would travel to Barnes to have a look around his room for any evidence of this surveillance, and travel on to Cambridge with my father. Being with him for hours on end didn't fill me with joy.

The week passed in a haze, I'd tried to catch up on a commission but my heart and any hope of focus was just not in it. I had two articles to write and I needed to finish off The Guardian piece but also write a column for an artist magazine which is for burgeoning painters. I sat in front of my computer screen staring at it as if creative thoughts would burst out of my very being. I found myself nodding off at one point. Only Cosmo was having a great time, he had no worries about money or the anxiety of life. I hadn't heard from my mother since the disastrous meeting although I hadn't really expected to. I know that I had touched on a raw subject but I honestly thought that it would probably bond him to her more closely. I didn't feel any guilt about asking her but I was just saddened at her response. Sebastian was only 18 years old, still a child really who still needed protecting but I guess she was just protecting herself. So, it was an awkward meeting when I arrived. We talked superficially over a coffee and then I made a quick exit up to Sebastian's room. I rifled through his drawers not feeling guilty anymore flicking through the journals and books for some sort of clue as to his fear of being under surveillance. I wasn't convinced of course that it was real but I felt a duty to Sebastian to look and Sophia was genuinely concerned.

It had been a few weeks since I had been in here, it was less shocking than before but disturbing nonetheless. I began to search for this supposed secret place, which seemed totally crazy. I had no idea what the hell I was looking for as I systematically looked through his belongings. Under the bed were plates still stained with food, clothes that smelled of sweat and urine and a collection of men's magazines with pages cut out or the models defaced. I left them how I found them. Everything I touched was odd, defaced or out of place and it wasn't until I was about to give up that I found a small plastic box, with his initials on the lid at the back of his wardrobe on the floor. I picked it up because it seemed to be covered in what looked like red paint. I opened the lid. I dropped it immediately and ran to the toilet to be sick.

.

IX

Once again my father and I sat across from Dr Trimbull.

"Your son has paranoid schizophrenia."

My father said nothing but started to breathe heavily, as he does, through his nose. I took the plastic box I'd found out of my pocket and placed it on the desk. "In here are two of Sebastian's teeth complete with gum and roots. I found the box at the back of his wardrobe, I think this was what Sebastian thought was a bugging device. I found a pair of blood stained pliers in his waste bin."

"You must try and understand that he has no ability to differentiate fact from fiction at this time. Paranoia is a major component, as the name suggests. He lives in a frightening world which often has no rhyme or reason. He has voices, one of God, telling him that he has to sacrifice himself for the greater good and angels telling him that he is God's son. We of course can see that his delusions are just that, delusions. Sadly the removal of these teeth, and he's not the first to do it, prove how deeply the psychosis has taken hold and how he must be protected from himself."

My father suddenly came to life, "How long is this going to last?"

"It's indeterminate. It's not like a physical illness where we can predict the duration, illnesses such as this cannot be dated and it's purely a matter of trial and error. We do have options to try. We can stick to one medication and ride it out until there is definitive improvement. We now need to have the Section 2 transferred to a Section 3 which is a six month treatment order."

"Six months, you must be joking right?" I blurted out.

"No, it gives us the chance to just treat the schizophrenia, a definite diagnosis which is often fudged in Section 2. We could try ECT but it is not normally used in psychotic illnesses but it is another option. He is not progressing as well as we had hoped. We haven't found a suitable drug yet and he is becoming more aggressive. We may have to consider transferring him to a secure unit."

"A secure unit? He didn't seem very aggressive when I saw him."

"As I understand it Mr Bradbury he tried to attack you but fortunately was restrained by his nurse. I am not saying that he is dangerous, at all, it's just he is fighting us all the way and a nurse or doctor may get hurt. He's making it very difficult to treat him. I know you talked to Hazel about transferring him closer to you but I would ere on the side of caution as private hospitals may not provide adequate acute care."

"So in the mean time we sit back on our laurels and wait."

"Yes, that's all we can do. You may have to come to terms with the fact that he's never going to be 100% better; it may be half that and he will take medication for the rest of his life."

"Can I see my brother now?"

"The ward manager will let you know if that's possible."

"So he definitely will not completely recover?"

"It is possible but for this type and severity of illness, the proportion of patients who recover completely is extremely low. We just have to hope for the best at this stage."

We didn't talk on our walk over to the ward; I think we were both numb from what had transpired. Sebastian had been sedated due to a confrontation earlier with

Errol, who was now diligently sitting in his usual place in the doorway of Sebastian's room. He was reading a newspaper, one eye on the football scores and the other on Sebastian's sleeping form. Sebastian was sleeping naked on the mattress on the floor his only warmth from a thin white NHS blanket covering his pale thin legs. My father stayed outside the room, there was no compassion or love in his eyes. He looked at him as if he was a homeless person living under a bridge in a cardboard box. He looked at Seb then at me and then walked off.

Instead of a chair I sat down beside him my legs crossed like a child in primary school. People always remark about watching people sleep, which I'd always thought to be odd and rather stalkerish, but that is exactly what I did. He looked helpless. Heaven only knows what was active in that brain of his. I must have sat there for at least 15 minutes before Melanie walked in.

"Hi Ben, I didn't see you come on the ward, how you doing?"

"Fine. Everything still going well?"

"It's great; I want to work here when I qualify. I saw my first ECT this morning, it was okay. I thought I'd be freaked out but it was really interesting. I've come to take Sebastian's blood pressure; I do it every 15 minutes. I really like your brother, I think some nurses are afraid of him but I've never had a problem, he's always been nice to me. He's lucky to have a brother like you. Do you want a more comfortable chair?"

"No it's okay I'm quite happy on the floor. How long has he been asleep?"

"A couple of hours I think, he was fighting against the sedation for the longest time. Well I'll be back in 15 min, I've got to take his BP again, I can't remember whether the meds increase or decrease it but they always say it's fine. I'll bring some more blankets as he may get cold."

So there we were, this was not what I had planned for, I wanted to be with him but before now I would have thought that it would be a futile exercise. Every now and then he'd mutter something inaudible and change position. If you have never watched a person sleep I highly recommend it, it's a very therapeutic experience. I had arrived for the meeting all irritable and anxious and now after sitting here I could feel my heart rate dropping and my breathing becoming more normal. Every so often Errol would look over and I would nod that everything was fine.

Hazel popped in before the end of her shift.

"Hey, Ben."

"How's he doing really? I keep getting no change when I ring. His doctor says that he's really no different."

"I know is frustrating. It takes time. He's spending a little more time awake than asleep now but Errol is still with him during the day and Savin, an agency nurse, is with him during the night. Sebastian is quite an active creature at night as are a lot of schizophrenics; he certainly keeps Savin on his toes."

"Do you think they will do ECT? I just don't like the sound of that at all."

"Possibly, but it is quite uncommon now to use it for psychosis. It is only used as a last resort. It's not like you see in the movies. Its painless, the patient is unconscious. It's strictly supervised. Most common downside is slight memory loss and of course it not being successful. I shouldn't worry about it now it is only a suggestion."

"And the sectioning?"

"Section 3 you mean? That's a definite at this stage. It can be rescinded at any point though; it could possibly be only two weeks after it is in place."

"My father wants him transferred to a private hospital near home."

"I know, he rang me a couple of days ago, I don't know if you know that and I spoke with Dr Trimbull."

"No. No I didn't."

"At the moment Sebastian's behaviour could warrant a transfer to a secure unit. That will be difficult to find in the private sector as I'm sure he told you. He can get quite aggressive and we have to think about the safety of our staff and other patients. When we have restrained him he's a tough cookie so he will be hard to place elsewhere. His safety is also of paramount importance, any transfer needs to be approached with level heads and extreme caution. He is not dangerous but he is a danger to himself. I tried to explain this to your father but he still feels strongly about moving him. Dr Trimbull just rang me about the teeth he pulled out. He warrants complete supervision as you can see. We even cannot risk taking him to a dentist; we don't even know if he is in pain. Perhaps you need to have a further discussion with your father outlining what we have talked about."

"I can't believe this is happening to him, he's a gentle kid you know."

"I know. He's lucky to have you."

"Yeah, right."

I spent another ten minutes sitting with him, until my legs could take the hard floor no longer. I was hoping he would wake up but he didn't. I left the ward with a smile though as I watched Melanie skipping down the ward seemingly blissfully happy. Sebastian was more than lucky to have her.

My father was sitting in the car listening to the depressing tones of Radio 4 and he didn't acknowledge my presence until I was doing up my seatbelt.

"You were a long time considering he was asleep."

"I just wanted to sit with him for a bit. Look can you drop me off in town; there is someone I want to see. I'll get a train back to Barnes later."

"I didn't know you knew anybody in Cambridge."

"I do."

He dropped me off at Sebastian's college and drove off without so much as a 'goodbye'. I of course made my way to Susan's office and she was more than a little surprised to see me.

"Hi, what are you doing here, have you just visited Sebastian?"

"Yes but I wanted to see you. Cosmo and I missed you. Shall I come back another time if you're busy?

"No, not at all. It's nice to know Cosmo missed me; is he eating you out of house and home? He reminds me of a pony I had as a child, it was called Bertrum, silly name huh?"

"I've been wanting to ring you since five minutes after I left you last week."

"Ben."

"Oh no I'm sorry, I should have called and now I've put you in a really awkward position. I have verbal diarrhoea when it comes to talking to women, not that I've have had that many women."

"Ben."

"Oh God now I'm just rambling."

"Ben, take a deep breath. I was just going to say that I need to finish up here. I'll be about an hour or so, so why not take these keys. Let yourself into my flat and make yourself at home."

"Great, I'll do that. I'll see you later then."

"About an hour and, Ben; don't think so much, try and relax."

It felt wonderful being in her flat again and sitting on that comfy sofa I was able for a few minutes to finally relax. I poured myself a whisky; I took my shoes off and turned on the telly. The complicated lives of those appearing on daytime talk shows just astounded me. Why would you air your dirty laundry in front of millions of viewers purely for entertainment purposes? Well I suppose it is just that, entertainment.

Susan arrived a couple of hours later and found me asleep on the sofa. She even managed to have a shower and make dinner while I slept like sleeping beauty. It wasn't long though into the meal that I poured out the whole day's events. And she certainly wasn't that bad a cook.

"So he's definitely schizophrenic?"

"Yep; paranoid schizophrenic. Bottled, labelled and most likely in the future to be discarded."

"Why do you say that? Is there no hope of him getting better?"

"He's on enough medication to kill a rhino; he's heavily sedated most of the day. He hates me; our parents don't seem to give a shit and he pulled out two of his back teeth with a pair of pliers because he thought they were bugging devices. I don't see much hope of a bright future for him. As for me, I'm living in a vacuum that is sucking me further in; I can't concentrate on work, I'm having dreadful nightmares and something is telling me that this is only the beginning."

"Do you think you might be in need of some sort of counselling?"

"You mean therapy? The staple American diet."

"Yeah, therapy. Think about it Ben. You have got to be able to cope with this and you are all by yourself. Your 22 years old, you shouldn't have to be dealing with your brother alone. I'm not a great believer in therapy, counselling, whatever they call it these days, but I can tell you're really suffering. You don't want to become so depressed that you can no longer look out for yourself. I can listen for however long it takes but I cannot help you learn to deal with it. I'm here for you but I see a guy of 22 sitting beside me who is rapidly becoming 40. Do you kinda understand where I'm coming from?

"Therapy huh? Never really thought about it. I was always led to believe that therapy was a sign of weakness. That's from my father's guidebook of life. Keep all problems to yourself. Keep that stiff upper lip he's so damn proud of."

"You're not your father. Just think about it. I can always ask if anyone knows anyone around here or perhaps you would prefer someone who is closer to your home. I don't want to see this situation just eat you alive. You need some self-preservation."

"I best be off soon, trains are so unreliable these days. I'll end up sleeping on the platform."

"Stay."

I must have paused for the longest time, making her feel terribly awkward.

"Sorry; bad timing. I've obviously read the signals wrong."

"No. No you haven't at all, I really find you incredibly attractive but..."

"It's the age difference isn't it? I must look like such a cradle snatcher or an old hag trying to get my claws into a guy who four years ago was still in school. I've put you in such an embarrassing position, I'm sorry."

"It's my own neuroses." A small part of me still held a torch for Sophia and the whole situation with Seb was just playing over and over in my head. My physical body cried out for physical affection and emotion, but my cerebral self declined. "I'm sorry I can't, not just now."

"You are allowed to say 'no' Ben. It's okay. I just feel that we have a connection, I totally understand if you don't feel the same way. It's not a problem. We can say that this conversation never happened."

My mind was confused: there was the typical rebound from previous girlfriend; there was the physical feeling of not having sex in a long time; the fact that I did not want to lead her on; whether those reasons were even true and the fact that she was far more experienced than I was in that department, and that I might be ashamed of my whole performance. Surprising myself I told her that.

"I'm afraid that I will not live up to your expectations and that you'll see me for what I am-a neurotic artist who is crap in bed."

She gave out a huge laugh, "Oh God is that all you are worried about? Do you think because I'm older than you that I'm going to be some sort of sexual guru who spurns all those who cannot satisfy me? I've had a handful of relationships, a couple serious, and you know how one of them turned out. It's not an issue that I hold high on my importance list. It's supposed to be fun and enjoyable right? It's not like choosing the best ride at Disneyland. You know that all people have different ways and sometimes you just have to keep going till you find out. You're not Rudolph Valentino who can please every woman in Hollywood and I'm not Marilyn Monroe. You just need to put that huge bag of anxiety on the floor for a while and do something that pleases you."

I was nervous, nervous as hell, as we lay there and inevitably what I feared would happen happened. The artist failed to deliver. I was Van Gogh but with different part of the anatomy cut off. I couldn't look at her. I sat at the end of the bed facing the door, ready to leap up and run away as far as I could but the fact that I was naked did limit how far I could go.

"Hey, it doesn't matter. It's no big deal. I think I kind of forced you into this."

"You didn't force me into anything. I think I need to go." I began to fumble into my clothes as she sat wrapped in the sheet watching me.

"It's 11.30 you'll never get back now. You can stay on the couch if you wish."

"I don't know if my humiliation can get even lower if I still sleep here."

"Don't be so silly. These things happen, it's quite normal. Please don't worry about it. Let's just talk, have a drink and see what happens."

"I'm sorry."

The instant I shut the front door behind me I regretted it. Where was I going? I had no idea. I just wandered the streets until I felt too tired to continue. I had nowhere to go except back to Susan's to endure the awkwardness of what had taken place. She was waiting up for me knowing that I would return. I didn't sleep on the couch as you could probably have guessed, I shared her bed. We laid side by side her head resting on my chest. I would have loved to have been able to draw her like this. She had the softest hair which tickled against my bare skin. I felt my body relaxing under her but my brain was awake and feverishly active.

My reoccurring dream began that night; the waitress, Venice and Sebastian. I woke up with a shout, shaking violently as if I had been in a washing machine. Susan awoke with my shout and after a few minutes of trying to alleviate my panic she held me close and soothed me back to sleep. Strangely I woke with a fresh sense of perspective and after a very satisfying and, thankfully, successful encounter with Susan and a hearty breakfast I made my way back to Barnes. I was smiling outrageously on the train ride home much to the amusement of two giggling schoolgirls who were seated opposite.

I arranged to meet her in a few days and in between those days I attempted to finish some work. I didn't need to worry about Cosmo as he was quite happy running continually up and down looking for a ball that we had lost when he came to me. I vowed to buy him another one the next time I was in town. My house, or rather cottage, sat alone in acres of land which ended at the sea. There was a small dirt track that led to a minor road into town and when living here I only ventured out to the town once a week the rest was spent in solitude. Over the four years we were together Sophia only spent a year actually living here. I never experienced loneliness but did on occasion crave some company. My friends were Sophia's friends and most of them lived in London.

Due to bad weather and the temptation to brace the outdoors I was able to knuckle down and write the two articles required for the magazines and I was so relieved they were out of the way. I'm an artist after all not a writer. There was a commission that I was unable to focus on as I felt extreme sadness when I picked up the brush; sadness over Sebastian and sadness over my own confusing situation, which wasn't dissipating as time was moving on. I thought about Susan's suggestion about therapy but balked at the idea, I was indeed my father's son.

Susan, to whom I was growing more and more attracted, was also a concern. We didn't live remotely near each other, I had no desire to move to Cambridge and I was also beginning to regret my sleeping with her despite my growing attachment. I felt guilty that I may have done it for all the wrong reasons. For the first time in four years after that one night I was beginning to feel alone. Not physically but emotionally and spiritually. I felt that I was just unloading my baggage onto her like she was a priest in the confession box. I hoped that this feeling would subside but it didn't.

The next time we met my feelings of doubt were still very much present and the older and wiser Susan picked up that feeling in me pretty quick.

"I know Ben that you have mixed feelings about us, in whatever capacity. I can read it in your face. You haven't decided who I am to you, whether I'm just a friend, a friend who you'd just like to fuck, although I suspect not, a lover, a therapist or your mother."

"You surely are not my mother."

"I'm not saying that is what you think but I can see you're confused. You're at a really vulnerable time just now so why don't we just be friends who enjoy each other's company. Later we might feel different but there is no reason for us to define anything. I love your company, accept it and let's just enjoy that for the time being."

I was silent for a long time; she didn't press for me to answer.

"I wondered what you thought about the counselling idea. I do have a number of one in Cambridge but it probably isn't where you'd want it to be. Just thought I'd research a little bit because I know you won't. Her name is Lynne Moretti; husband is Italian I think. Here's the number."

I took the piece of paper. "Thanks but I'm still not sure."

"Hey, it's just a number. Can I visit Sebastian with you? I'd like to see him."

"It's probably not a good idea as it may be an unpleasant experience. I'll meet you later."

"I'll just keep you company I can stay in the car."

"What about work?"

"I'm off to see a student!"

"If you are sure."

"I'm a big girl so yes I'm sure."

She found my car rather amusing and it was the first time I'd ever been embarrassed about it. I thought it was rather quirky and artiste like. Now it seemed a bit ridiculous. She suggested we take her car; trying to persuade me that it was because there was more room in hers. She possessed a BMW, which surprised me as I'd always had a warped theory about BMW drivers, that they were always aggressive drivers who tailgate you on motorways. I refrained from sharing my theory with her however. But I have to confess it was a more comfortable and smoother ride.

I felt pangs of guilt as I asked her to remain in the car as I believed it was too soon for him to have any other visitors at that time. He didn't recognise me so I didn't want to upset him anymore than necessary. She just smiled and turned on the radio. As I was buzzed onto the ward, my levels of anxiety began to rise. Was I still afraid of my own brother?

I spotted Hazel in the office, "Hi Hazel, how is he today?"

"Well he's awake for you today. He wasn't happy this morning as Errol and a couple of other nurses gave him a bath. There was a fight but Errol won. One of the nurses thought they saw lice so we couldn't risk it with other patients. He's still refusing to wear clothes but that's the last of our worries, and what's more he's confined to his room anyway."

"Is he taking his medication?"

"Off and on. We're not having to resort to injecting him as much but it does vary from day to day. I informed your father this morning that he was placed on a Section 3 and we have far more scope in dealing with the hygiene issues as well as the other problems. Sebastian's erratic behaviour has calmed down considerably so a secure unit is not required for the moment; that's not to say he might not in the foreseeable weeks. He's on-one-to one nursing all the time still but I'm sure you'll find him a little improved. Night time is still difficult for him, he believes he's being invaded by, well I'm still not quite sure what, when he's asleep. As you can imagine he's terrified and he screams a lot but he still fights against any medication we try to give him. But there is an improvement even if it doesn't sound like it. Go see him."

I was used to the ward now, the strangeness of the environment and the patients. Sebastian's immediate neighbour was a young girl, around Sebastian's age, with bi-polar disorder who was currently in the grip of mania. She was flouncing around the ward in a bikini and towel wrapped around her waist; like she was in the Wham! Club Tropicana video. Like Melanie, she skipped along the corridor sending out happy carefree vibes to all those she came in contact with. She cheerfully approached me and proceeded to hand me an origami rose.

"You're his brother aren't you? Sebastian's brother."

"Yeah, my name is Ben."

"I've made you this, you looked sad the last time you were here. I'm going to make a whole garden so it will be summer all year round."

"That's really nice, it is very pretty."

"Have you got a girlfriend because I could be your girlfriend?"

"No and I don't really want one just now but I appreciate your gesture."

"Sebastian's really crazy I can hear him screaming at night. I like him. Well see you."

She turned around very gracefully and danced off. I didn't know whether to feel sorry for her or envious of her oblivion to her situation. The conversations with Sarah did become more lucid over the next few visits. She was older than I expected, she was 26 and was a dispatcher for the emergency services. As I approached Sebastian's door I could see Errol, posted as usual in the doorway looking exceeding bored. I could hear talking and laughing but Errol was not conversing back.

"Hi Errol. Is there someone with him?"

"No, just him. Don't worry about it he's just responding to the voices he hears in his head. Just ignore it and don't question them. He's fine, you can go in. Sebastian you have a visitor."

Sebastian was seated naked in his usual Buddha lotus position on the floor with a thin covering of blanket. The room was chilly but he didn't seem to be affected by it. The mattress on the floor still remained but was now covered in what looked like fresh linen. The bed frame had been removed and so had a small chest of drawers. One chair and the mattress remained. It looked worse than I imagined a prison cell would look like.

With trepidation I called his name.

"Oh look, it's Benjamin. To what do I owe this pleasure?"

Errol had now stood and had his arms crossed which did alarm me it must be said. "Tell him what you told me earlier Sebastian."

"That you're my brother."

I could have easily wept right then, "Yeah, you're absolutely right. You're my little brother. Can I sit next to you? I would have liked to have bought you something but I didn't know what you would like."

"God provides everything I need. I have everything I need right here."

Just seconds after saying this he suddenly smiled and muttered something completely inaudible. I looked to Errol who held up a hand and shook his head to stop me asking I assume what he was laughing at. "How are you doing?"

"They forced water over my body."

"So I see, I think it's a good look."

"Do you?"

"Yeah, even Jesus probably washed once in a while. Didn't he get baptized in the River Jordan? It would have been very difficult to do that without getting wet."

"So, you know all about me? Just like they do; those who follow?"

"I know that your name is Sebastian Bradbury, you are 18 years old; you study astrophysics at Cambridge..."

"Continue."

"You broke your arm age 12 falling out of an apple tree in our garden. At school you used to wear your blazer inside out..."

"That's an interesting fiction. Do you know about the people who are following me? The people who control us by bugging us but I was smart and got rid of them. I took them out. They couldn't get near me before but I know they are here now. They come through the walls; they are in the walls right now. Go and listen you can hear them. Listen."

I wasn't sure whether to do as he asked and looked helplessly at Errol. He shrugged his shoulders.

"Where were the bugging devices, how did you know they were?"

"I could feel them in my teeth. I could taste them, they were leaking through my body and entering all my other organs. I can feel them moving around especially at night. The people come out at night, Benjamin, you must watch out."

I was now paranoid about my own teeth; I kept running my tongue over them ensuring they were still there. His paranoia was transferring onto me. "Are you in pain? Your teeth? Will you show me where you took them out so I'll be able to check mine?"

He opened his mouth and I leaned forward to look at what he'd done to himself. At the very back I could see a large ugly space where he had ripped the teeth out with the pliers. It looked terribly sore and in my limited knowledge of dentistry not completely healed. "That looks really sore."

"All for the greater good. If I can survive them so can others. You are in danger too. You must become an angel like I'm going to be."

"I'm not good with heights and flying. Angels have to fly don't they?"

"I can protect you."

Again he had a moment in his own head where he seemed preoccupied and began to giggle. I watched him with fascination as he had a conversation intermittently with himself. I began to struggle again with all this. He seemed worse than when he was first taken to hospital. I understood that it may happen but it was hard to comprehend it when it happened. I was unspeakably happy that I had managed to regain our connection but heartbroken when I began to see what his future life would be if this insidious illness didn't leave him. While with him I tried to remain upbeat and retain normal conversation.

"Do you have good food here, better than my cooking?"

"I have no interest in food; angels require no food apart from air. They make me eat here; I always try to spit it out."

"You need food to live. You must get hungry. Dad would like to come and see you would you like that?"

"God visits me every day."

"That's nice but I'm sure Father would like to see you." He drifted off again and I was beginning to feel I was struggling with conversation. I was therefore pleased that a nurse I didn't know came in with what looked like medication.

"Medication time Sebastian."

"Not today thank you. I'm going to use prayer. I'll pray for you Paul."

"That ain't happening Sebastian. You can pray all you want but you still have to take your meds. Do you want this to be done the easy way or the hard way?"

"God will forgive you."

Paul, I sensed, had no patience for Sebastian's behaviour so I intervened.

"Hey, why don't you take it and then we can continue to talk? There's no reason for them to do it any other way. Take it while I'm here."

"No, they are trying to poison me. I must be careful. You know better than that Paul. They are not going to get me."

"Okay Sebastian. You're not getting another chance after this. You took it yesterday what is wrong with today. You don't want to upset your brother do you?"

"Benjamin is at peace with himself, you may do unto me what you do to others."

Paul strode out on a mission to rectify the situation and I didn't want to be here when he returned. "I've got to go now Seb."

"You should stay for the show."

I heaved myself off the floor, my right leg giving way causing me to lose my balance a little. I definitely needed to work out at the gym as my body felt like it was 50. "I don't want to see that."

Paul returned with a small cup and a dish containing a syringe. "This is the last opportunity to take it orally."

"No thank you. You do what you need to do and I'll do what I need to do. I'm sure Benjamin agrees with me. He knows you've been poisoning me."

"No-one is poisoning you, you know that."

Sebastian closed his eyes, back in the world inside his head.

"Now would be a good time to leave Mr Bradbury."

"Yes, of course. Bye Seb see you soon."

I quickly left nearly running into two more nurses waiting in the corridor. I pulled the exit door open and then heard the scream. I almost forgot about Susan who was waiting so patiently in the car, "I'm sorry if I was a long time. I said it would be boring for you."

"How was he?"

"He knows I'm his brother..."

"Oh that's great.... I can see a 'but' right around the corner..."

"He thinks he's being poisoned and being spied on. He's completely deluded, refusing to take his meds. I thought he would be at least a little better but he's more delusional than before he went in. I just don't understand it. Look sorry, here I am dumping my baggage on you again. How about we get some lunch?"

We dined at the restaurant where we first went and I managed to refrain from bringing Sebastian's name or situation into the conversation. She talked about her interest in photography and travel; it transpired that we had the same love of Italy. I spoke of Sophia, her family and of Montepulciano. The conversation flowed easily as we shared stories of our childhoods and terrible teenage years. I made her laugh with the stories of Seb and our horse Percy when we were growing up and how he used to drink pints of Guinness and packets of crisps when my grandfather used to take him to the pub. Percy was a gypsy pony, tethered to the side of the road when my grandfather paid to take him off the gypsies' hands. He was an incredibly photogenic black and white cob, all mane and feathers, who would always try and please and who loved to pose for a photo. We both learnt to ride on him, but sometimes we didn't progress that far as he'd far rather park himself in a spot of grass and eat. After my grandfather's death he was sold to a really lovely gregarious lady, a writer, who showered him in love from the moment she saw him. We drew comfort from the fact that he had gone on to a good home. Our grandparents were very different from our parents as they were very generous with their time and in their love. Sadly all our grandparents had died before I reached my 16th birthday.

Susan was considerably well travelled and had been to places like: Borneo to photograph the orang-utans; China to see the pandas and to Jordan to see the magnificence of what is Petra. I was incredibly envious and somewhat ashamed of my pathetic attempts to see the world. I'd been to Italy, of course, other European cities and also had the misfortune to visit Los Angeles to stay with a school friend. It was far removed from the preconceived vision I'd had of it and I was very disappointed. The whole area which makes up LA is vast and as we had no method of transportation it made leaving the vicinity of Los Feliz very difficult. Having no car in LA is like having no legs. It was an experience nonetheless but one I didn't wish to repeat. As she spoke, I watched her perfectly formed mouth and noticed the whiteness of her incredibly straight teeth. I had a sudden flashback of looking at the gaping hole is Sebastian's mouth and as I tried to focus on her words, I watched her mouth move but did not hear the sound that was coming out. It was like I had become deaf or was in a nightclub with music playing so loud that you couldn't hear yourself speak.

I don't know how long we had been talking but I knew I had to get out of there. I was being suffocated by my own thoughts, "I'm sorry, I've got to go."

"Ben, what's wrong?"

"I've just got to get out of here now." I started to breathe heavily and could feel my heart pounding so hard that I thought it might break through my rib cage. My whole body started to shake and beads of sweat were trickling down my forehead. I thought at that moment I was going to die.

"Let me get the bill and we will go okay?"

It seemed like it was forever before we were finally outside. The fresh air hit me like speeding train. I must have looked so stupid to the passers-by in the street, pacing and trying desperately not to cry. Susan attempted to hold my hand trying her best to deal with the, now embarrassing, situation.

"It's okay; it's okay. Take a deep breath." If you have ever tried to calm a person in distress you will know how hard it is to get the person to breathe deeply. It's a completely futile exercise and I just wasn't listening. Next thing I remember I woke up on the concrete pavement lying on my side, even more terrified than before. By now I had gathered quite a crowd around me but believe it when I say that you just don't care. Susan was knelt down beside me, holding my hand along with an older gentleman that I didn't know. My head felt fuzzy and I felt really cold, probably due to the cold pavement I was lying on. I could hear the sound of an ambulance in the background but it took a while to register that it was for me.

"Ben, can you hear me? Ben!"

I managed to focus my gaze on her.

"Hey, just lie still. You're okay. There is an ambulance on its way. Everything is going to be okay."

They say those lines so often in movies that it sort of sounds cheesy and predictable but it is probably the most natural thing in the world to say and it is, from first-hand experience quite comforting and reassuring. The ambulance arrived and more of a crowd had developed and the gentleman beside me was, luckily, a retired doctor. There is nothing more pleasing than having the right person at the right time. I felt like my lungs had stopped working and I was drowning. I was administered oxygen by the ambulance crew which was like nectar and before I had a chance to say anything I was on my way to hospital.

Diagnosis: panic attack. The first of many. It was no surprise given all the stress of the last few weeks and I was released after a couple of hours into Susan's capable hands. I was unaccountably embarrassed by the whole affair. Susan was anxious about my driving home and offered to drive me back to my parents. "Look I'm so sorry; I'm just a neurotic mess."

"Maybe but you're one hell of a cute mess!"

I had to smile, the first time in many days. I was falling in love with her; more and more over the time we spent together. She seemed unfazed by the impending meeting with my mother, my father, in a social situation. I assumed father would not have returned from work when we were due to arrive. Despite my mother's questioning of her, Susan held her own and I even saw my mother soften and bring down some of those protective barriers she was famous for. Susan was the one who bought up the afternoon's events but was visibly taken aback by my mother's lack of feeling at this. I was beginning to wish I had had a heart attack to at least get some sort of sympathetic reaction. My father had still not returned from work when Susan made her move to go back to Cambridge. Her living there was becoming a rather large obstacle in our burgeoning relationship.

XI

Lynne Moretti. Her business card was in my hand. It had been a couple of days since my panic attack and I had kept picking up this card and putting it down without doing anything. She was based in Cambridge but of course so was Susan. After I had spent a few hours in the studio I drew all the courage I could possibly muster and picked up my phone but after one ring I pressed cancel. What was I afraid of? I didn't know. It was just a phone call. So I rang again and this time it went to answerphone. I was relieved on the one hand but I hate leaving messages so the message left was from a stuttering idiot. Now all I had to do was worry effortlessly until she rung back.

Cosmo needed a walk and so did I. The seashore can be such a lonely place but for an artist it can bring inspiration and feelings of great passion. You may find it difficult to believe that vast quantities of sand and water can bring such emotions but humans are a mere speck in comparison to sand and sea. Nature owns our planet not human beings and there is something very powerful and emotive about that.

Cosmo was so carefree and marvelled at the smallest insignificant things; at one point he tried to outsmart a crab as it scuttled back into the sea; then ran rings around me urging me to throw non-existent items for him to catch. He was not so much a sea dog though as every time he reached the edge of the water and a small ripple of wave approached him he would scamper back to me for refuge. We very rarely met others walking on the beach but today we encountered two horse riders, majestic, proud on powerful animals cantering in the shallow waves. God certainly pushed the boat out when he created horses. I don't believe Cosmo had ever seen a horse before and started to bark and get overexcited. I pulled him close to me and made him sit as the horses went by and I heard a soft message of thanks as they cantered past and into the distance.

A message had been left on my phone but I chose to ignore it until I was completely panic-free. When all panic had subsided I picked up the phone pressed the call button, screwed my eyes up tightly and hoped for the best.

"Lynne Moretti?"

"Yes."

"I'm Ben Bradbury, I left you a message."

"Oh yes. When would you like to meet with me?"

I needed to think fast as I would need the time to drive up to Cambridge. "I can come in the afternoon any week day is fine." Friday at two was the arranged time. That way I'd have time to drive to Cambridge, have lunch and also spend time with Susan. She seemed nice on the phone but that doesn't really say much. I felt pathetic and rather sorry for myself so I got drunk and somehow got to bed.

I woke up with a start and in a cold sweat again after dreaming of Sebastian in Venice. I got up this time and walked around my room trying to take those deep breaths I'm not good at doing. I opened the window and stuck my head out breathing in the fresh air. I must have been standing there for around 5 to 10 minutes when I finally felt my vital signs return to normal. I couldn't face going back to bed so I went into my studio. I began to paint slowly methodically at first then furiously as if my hand was possessed with some sort of demon. My mind was so focused that nothing else mattered. What was I painting? I did not know. Large strokes of black and yellow covered the canvas. There was no rhythm or rhyme to the brush but I continued on until my hand began to ache. I stood back and breathed in my nightmare masterpiece. It consisted of streaks and circles of colour, nothing more; no subliminal messages or heavenly symbols. Perhaps I was hoping that it would suggest some miraculous vision that would enlighten me. Even Cosmo looked unimpressed.

Cosmo made it clear he was hungry; I hadn't felt hungry in weeks. Coffee was my staple diet. I had a shower, looked at my emails and waited until 9am to phone the ward. I phoned religiously at this time and I'm sure the ward staff were sick of me but I really didn't care anymore. The usual response was 'he's doing fine' but I never believed them so I usually rang back and spoke to Hazel to satisfy my own sanity.

Friday: I was beginning to regret the phone call to Lynne Moretti. I had spoken to Susan the day before and she was a little too excited about my impending therapy session. I felt like I was crazy and she was confirming it. The journey to Cambridge was non eventful and I arrived for the appointment ten minutes early and sat in the car waiting for my anxiety levels to reach their maximum. Her house was a small terraced house in a fairly quiet street and any nosey neighbour would see strangers coming to and fro throughout the day and draw their own conclusions. At 1.58 I was knocking on her door.

The door opened and what seemed like a Siberian husky escaped out the door. Its owner, a woman of small stature, thick curly hair and olive skin whom I assumed to be Ms Moretti tried to coax it back into the house. She was definitely a lady of Italian or Mediterranean origin.

It was a comical scene as there I stood all 6ft 1 and she of around 5ft. I wondered whether to kneel down.

"Ben? Hope you like dogs. Hippy is very friendly despite his size."

Hippy was an incredibly beautiful looking dog; huskies have that wolf look in their facial features and this dog seemed like the blueprint for their breed, "I've got one myself not so stunning though." I was led through to a small room which was cosy yet practical. I always wondered what therapist's consulting room looked like. I sat down uneasily in the nearest chair and on the table beside me sat a glass of water and a box of Kleenex.

"Coffee? Tea?"

"Um no. No thank you."

"You may find it a little more relaxing if you do and you're not just being polite."

I gave a little smile, she knew me even before I sat down. "Tea, just black, thanks." I noticed the bookcase behind me and it was full of psychiatric books: 'Living in Fear', 'Suicide the Facts', 'Free your inner child' and other cheery subjects.

"So what brings you to me Ben?"

I shuffled in the seat, "I'm not sure. I really didn't want to. Really didn't."

"So why have you come?"

"I supposed I've been pushed into it by a friend. She thinks I should see someone."

"Why does she think so?"

"She thinks I'm going to fall apart and be depressed."

"Do you feel depressed?"

I said no, knowing that my world was becoming unmanageable but one thing I was certain of was that

I would not be sharing with this woman no matter how hard she pushed. My pride and upbringing would not allow it. My awkwardness became more apparent as I shifted restlessly in my seat. She obviously saw my discomfort.

"Would you like to continue or do you want this to go no further?"

"My brother's crazy," I heard myself say out loud. "He's in a mental hospital and he's been diagnosed schizophrenic. Found out just last week. He thought he could fly off his university roof." I gave a huge sigh of relief as if a huge secret I was unable to keep had burst out unintentionally.

"And you're angry about that?"

I felt my anxiety rising as I began opening up to this complete stranger and I had a moment of reflection before I made the decision to answer. "Not at him but the shit we've been dealt with. I'm working my ass off earning a living and I'm having to be brother, mother and father to my fucked up 18 year old brother. Yeah, that I'm angry about. I'm a sinking ship and everyone close to me is jumping off."

"What do you mean everyone?"

"Our parents have near disowned both of us, my girlfriend of four years bailed on me and I have a friend who thinks I'm going just as mad as my brother."

"You smiled when you said that."

"Because I keep thinking someone is going to wake me up and shout 'surprise!'"

"Like a joke?"

"Yeah, or maybe it's God just effing around." My body was still tense and the more I talked the more tense I became. What the hell was therapeutic about that?

What followed was an uncomfortable silence for a few minutes perhaps more. I sat and stared at the floor while Lynne sat comfortably in her chair; hands placed together as though she was praying and stared at me waiting for my next revealing utterance. In the end I couldn't bare the silence.

"I keep having the same dream." She just nodded encouraging me to continue, "I'm in Venice, sitting in a café and a young waitress who is flirting with me turns out to be my brother Sebastian; but he's laughing hysterically, like a crazy person. It disturbed me before; frightened me you know what I mean? But now it just fills every dream I have and is a constant reminder of my duty to him. I can't get him out of my head."

"What duty do you think you have to him?"

"Who is going to take care of him?"

"He may get better, as you said to me earlier it has only been a few weeks and he may in the future have an independent life. Is that a possibility?"

"I don't know. I don't think so, his doctor isn't that optimistic, but you see films and read in the papers about schizophrenics living in doorways and living in shelters, murdering people and ending up in prison. I don't want to see him like that; I couldn't live with myself if that happened. I can't run away from him, I have no option to. I can't work, I can't sleep."

"Have you spoken with your parents about how all this is affecting you?"

I gave a huge sigh of resignation and defeat but could feel a bubbling of anger surfacing, "They are totally cut off from him and me. They're wallowing in their own vat of self-absorption to fully understand what's going on.

I don't want to resent my brother like I do my parents as he doesn't deserve it."

"It seems to me your real issue with this situation is something you're not bringing up."

I sunk further into the chair praying that these 50 minutes had come to an end. "I don't know what to say in response to that."

"What about guilt?"

She hit the nail on the head with that question and I couldn't avoid it. "Of course I feel bloody guilty. I visited home frequently when Seb was studying for his exams. He didn't talk and I didn't really make an effort, I laughed at the ridiculousness of his believing in aliens and his fear of being taken away. I just accepted it; we all did without any real concern. He was sleeping in a urine soaked bed, didn't wash and we just brushed it aside as a peculiarity of his. Who for Christ's sake doesn't do something, anything, about that? I don't that's who. I'm filled to the brim with guilt that I didn't do something sooner. He was scared shitless, alone and lived in his bedroom for safety; while I was living a productive and enjoyable life with someone I truly loved he lived in nothing but fear. Tell me that you wouldn't feel guilty about that?"

"You said you only visited home, isn't it too much to expect of yourself when you are not looking after him at these times. Some of that guilt should be lifted from your shoulders don't you think?"

I said nothing in response believing that she had no idea of what was going on or what I was feeling. I stared straight ahead avoiding eye contact with her.

"Your parents are where?"

"Living their own cosseted life in London; oblivious. Our mother hasn't even visited him yet and our father is giving him a very wide berth. He's just a kid, he needs his mum. What kind of mother doesn't want to be with their child when they are suffering? My mother had puerperal psychosis when Sebastian was born, she nearly drowned him in the bath, and she spent a couple of months in a psychiatric hospital, private of course, I only found this out recently. It's like she can't bear to be with him."

"So your mother has been through a lot."

"My mother is not a compassionate or affectionate woman. I'm not going to feel sorry her if that's what you are suggesting. She's had 18 years to deal with her own issues but she chooses to visit them on Sebastian instead. My father, well let's just say he'd rather be in a courtroom than with his own children."

And that was it, the fifty minute hour had ceased. I felt drained and needed a stiff drink. I felt far angrier than I've ever felt in my life. Is this what they mean when people say you've got to feel worse before you get better?

XII

The next few weeks passed without incident. I visited Sebastian when I came up for the weekend to stay with Susan. Our relationship was getting stronger but I still had my doubts about it being a long term thing. Not living in the same county was still a barrier. I needed to remain in Sussex and she in Cambridge, so as it was we only met at weekends. Sebastian was improving slowly and the one-to-one nursing had ceased during the day but continued at night when his psychosis seemed to be more prevalent. He occasionally refused his medication but was now willing to be persuaded. He was far from the model patient but caused no trouble for ward staff or other patients.

A clean shaven and washed brother was what I was greeted with now on my visits but it certainly wasn't a voluntary wash. He still sat crossed legged on the floor, slept on a bare mattress, wore minimal clothing and still believed he was Jesus. Apart from that you could now at least hold a conversation, albeit an often bizarre one, with him. He was allowed out for an hour with a nurse every day to walk to the park or to go to a café. As those trips out were successful, on my next visit I was allowed to take him out for an hour. He was due to be released from hospital in a few weeks. But then the unimaginable happened.

The day had started well enough; I'd returned from a walk with Cosmo; I had managed to paint for the first time in weeks and Susan and I were taking a short break to Amsterdam the following morning. Things were looking up in the Benjamin world. I had gone into town in the afternoon and on my return was greeted by the bleeping of my answer phone. Rather than check I simply closed the door and made myself a coffee, read my emails and had a bath.

The message however turned out to be urgent. It had been left three times. 10 minutes later I was driving to Cambridge. Hazel wouldn't explain over the phone what was wrong but I knew it was bad news.

Hazel tried to explain but I was numb. I saw her mouth move but I didn't hear anything at first. "What happened?" I finally said after I felt my mind flick back into function mode, "How is he? Where is he?"

Sebastian had stabbed himself in the eye, as written in the passage in the Book of Mark that he had highlighted in his bible at home.

"He had emergency surgery this afternoon but I'm afraid they couldn't save the eye. He's on a general ward for the night. I'm sorry this is a lot to take in…"

"How the hell did it happen? You're supposed to be looking after him …"

"There was a problem we did not foresee when he had an escorted trip out."

Sebastian had gone out for his hour's leave with a support worker, someone with no knowledge of psychiatry. These workers assist the nurses on the wards and are by large are a valuable asset in the spending of quality time with patients. Sebastian was not considered an absconding risk, a danger to himself or to others when he requested to go out. It transpired that Sebastian wanted to go to a local café. The choice of café by the worker would prove to be a massive, near fatal, mistake for it was a Christian coffee shop attached to a church which was run by devout Christian volunteers. Sebastian's religious proclivities were still very much a part of him and his psychosis and the worker after the incident happened claimed ignorance of this fact. Not only was the place a problem but she too was a devout Christian and carried a small bible in her handbag.

Surrounded by religious paraphernalia and a nurse who sat beside him as, he drank his tea, reading a bible proved far too much for his vulnerable mind to handle. According to the worker after 15 minutes or so of 'normal' behaviour, he stood up unexpectedly, exclaimed he was Jesus, pointed his finger at the terrified volunteers, preaching that they were all sinners and that they would be, like him, punished for their sins. The frightened and shocked worker could not prevent what happened next. As he was a lad over 6ft and she a small statured woman with no training and indeed limited physical strength she could do nothing but watch. He dashed to the counter where the cutlery was and grabbed a knife. He began to quote bible passages verbatim and then ceremoniously stabbed himself in the right eye and cut his face numerous times. According to the worker there was horrific screaming from those nearby but no wailing, screaming or crying from Sebastian. A passer-by alerted by the noise phoned the police and by the time they and the ambulance crew arrived it was all over. My brother had by then run into the church and was found kneeling with outstretched arms at the altar with the poor woman looking helplessly on, impotent in carrying out her duties. It took three police officers to restrain him as the ambulance crew worked trying to stabilise the bleeding. The shaken support worker accompanied him to hospital but was relieved of her duty shortly after. I just could not comprehend how they had allowed some religious nut to escort a schizophrenic 18 year old on an outing to a church.

Surgeons were unable to save his eye and I was just in total shock and bloody angry that he had been admitted to hospital with psychosis but was now facially disfigured. There were options of course, a glass eye for aesthetic purposes, but he was in no condition to make a choice. He was put in a private room off a general men's ward and now had two nurses, male of course, with him constantly. We were right back to square one and any previous improvement had been negated by this incident. This incident was the only time when I wanted to use my father's legal experience to sue the hospital's arse off.

The general ward was just as nasty as the psych wards, just as filthy and depressing. Sebastian's room was guarded by two nurses, one of which was Errol, who had been with Sebastian at the beginning of his stay on the psych ward, and another nurse, just as huge as Errol, whom I didn't know. Errol nodded in recognition and pushed the door open for me. Sebastian was lying awake curled up on his side on the bed. His right eye was covered over and a large dressing covered his right cheek.

"Sebastian. How are you doing?"

"Okay. I don't like it here. It smells funny."

"Yeah I know. You won't be here long. Sebastian, why did you hurt yourself?"

"I heard God's voice and I had to do it. We were at the church, my home, and I felt something enter my body, like a spirit. It was God. I looked all around me Ben and I saw destruction and death everywhere and we as human beings need to eliminate that from our world to create a peaceful place. We have no room for sinners and we must be punished for those sins. It's God's plan. I must suffer from my transgressions."

"Have you been taking your medication Seb?"

"I don't need that poison which they try and feed me."

"So you've been hiding it?"

"It's a very clever sleight of hand, any magician can do it. You can hide the pill in between your fingers by moving it from your palm and then pretend it is in your mouth. I can teach you if you like."

"How long have you been doing it?"

He smiled mischievously, "Quite a while now. I feel much better."

I felt like I was a hamster in a wheel, just peddling furiously going nowhere. I had had enough. I walked out the room, out the building and continued walking until my legs could take no more.

XIII

I did not return to Cambridge for a couple of weeks. I hadn't seen Susan either in that time. Our trip to Amsterdam was put on hold and she rang most days, sometimes I answered sometimes not, but I remained cocooned in my cottage in solitude, oblivious to the goings on in the world. Depression was hanging over me like a cloak. I couldn't sleep and I couldn't work. I got up at midday watched daytime television, ate occasionally then went back to bed. My mother phoned once and I put on the mask of positivity when I just wanted to just curl up and die. It was over a week before I ventured out of the house. Cosmo had been left to his own devices in the garden rather than on the beach and I had no fresh air in a long time. My head was still fuzzy and confused at what was happening to me but the break away from Sebastian was proving to be a positive one.

I swallowed the fresh air, taking vast gulps as I walked along the beach. I felt I was finally beginning to regain some semblance of my sanity. Once back in the house I cleared away all the dirty dishes that had been left on the floor over the past weeks and cleaned myself up. I also answered the phone in five days. It was Susan and she wasn't happy with me

"Ben, why the hell haven't you rang me or answered the phone? I've been worried sick, it's been five days."

"I've been a little preoccupied, and if you want to you can jump into my nightmare because the water is already warm."

"What are you talking about?"

"Sebastian stabbing himself in the eye. How much more crap is coming my way? I don't want you involved with this; it's too much to ask of you."

"I am the judge of that, you can't make that decision for me; it is unfair. How is he?"

"I haven't seen him since that day. He stopped taking his meds and he's completely nuts; what else can I say? So, I've been wallowing in self-pity in front of the television being a slob."

"I've got a few days off, I thought I'd come and see you, if you like, spend some quality time together. What do you say? At least say something Ben."

"What do you want me to say?"

"Yes or great or perfect, pick an adjective."

"Look, everything is just falling apart at the moment I'm just......I'm just trying to keep my shit together. I don't know if you coming down here is the best idea."

"Okay, I understand. I'm just trying to be supportive and I'm here if you need me. That's all I'm saying. I thought you could also use the company, your withdrawing into yourself more and more, it's not easy for me. I don't know what you want."

"I don't know what I want."

"You've got to bite the bullet and speak to your parents. They are responsible for him; you are not. You've got a life to lead and it's not as his carer. You'll end up in a ward with him if you carry on like this. Have you seen Lynne again?"

"No, I was even more depressed and anxious when I left than when I went in. Now I have even more things to worry about."

"Just let me come down and see you, we could have some fun, you need some fun."

"I don't know... I'm not good company."

"Come on Ben, you need to get out of this negative place your in."

"I know; it's not easy."

"I'm not saying it is but you can at least let me in, as a friend. Why go through all this alone? You don't need to have that stiff upper lip that you told me your father expects."

"Fine, you win. I'll see you on Saturday."

"I'll be there at 12 so you can take me out for lunch."

XIV

Nothing came of the investigation of the ward staff or the hospital. A risk assessment was carried out by his doctor and the ward staff and it concluded that he was no danger to himself or others and could leave the hospital for short periods of time. Susan and I continued with our weekend visits and, although I did have the worry that the relationship was becoming like Sophia and mine in terms of frequency of togetherness, I battled against my negative feelings and was now beginning to finally enjoy our relationship.

A month or so after the blinding incident, Sebastian was finally released from hospital into my parents' care for the time being. Other avenues such as supported housing and a group home were discussed in the final ward meeting before he was released. I couldn't bear the thought of him living in a bedsit somewhere alone even though the thought of him moving back to my parents' wasn't a positive one either. He had been in hospital for four months which felt like years to me. My parents knew that the once college-boy would become a massive responsibility and once again, like having a child, his needs would be greater than theirs.

Our father had softened slightly over the months and towards the end had played a more active role in his well-being. That is not to say that he had become like one of those happy families in the nauseating American sitcoms but he did try. He learnt the names of the ward staff and on two occasions took Sebastian out to the patient garden. Mother remained quite distant and did not visit him at all throughout his hospitalization. We never spoke again of her experiences with her own battle with mental health. Practically however she decided to make changes to the house and in particular to

Sebastian's room. She called me to come up and clear his room before the decorators moved in.

Once through the door a foul stale smell pervaded the air. I threw open the window but it took ages for the smell to start to even dissipate. It took hours to remove the various papers from the walls and I was glad to see them at home in the bin. I bound the personal journals from his desk and placed them in a box. I couldn't throw away years of my brother's life with one sweep into the bin. Underneath the bed I discovered a battered photograph album, full of family photos over the last 20 years. The front page was ripped out; the only evidence left, the rough edges of an angry tear.

The photos began with me as a baby held by my mother, bursting with pride, all those hours of labour forgotten. I looked like an alien, a huge headed baby. It was my Aunt Helen who held Sebastian in the next photo and the next and the next. My mother did not feature with Sebastian until he was a toddler. Pages after those had been torn out or defaced. Sebastian had cut out with a pair of pinking shears every face. These photos were of our adolescence and had featured our bad haircuts, bad skin and braces. I was in two minds as to whether I should throw it away but I didn't; it accompanied the journals to their new home in the attic.

As I continued to sort through his things a wave of depression came over me. Our unhappy childhood, I understood now, was a weight that was preying upon me. We weren't neglected as children but we weren't truly loved either. I had a group of friends in whom I trusted completely and whose families welcomed me in. The happiest time for me was when I was with them. My first trip parentless abroad was to Ibiza, student paradise, when we were in the sixth form. John was probably the closest to me; Harries, Andrew and George were the best mates imaginable. George and Andrew were amazingly close and spoke and acted as one; they even had their own code but you never felt like you were crashing their party.

I experienced my first joint at George's 18th birthday party. I don't remember much about it after the initial puff but embarrassingly I threw up on George's sister and passed out on their bathroom floor. I woke up hours later with remnants of shag pile in my mouth. After that though I became more immune to its effects and became a regular partaker in the stuff during university.

Naturally five lads let loose on holiday are going to run into some trouble. George and Andrew used to disappear for a few hours, seeking adventure of their own, while the three of us stayed in bed nursing hangovers. It didn't come as a surprise when one time George rang from the local hospital informing us that Andrew tried to pick up a girl on the beach and her body building boyfriend didn't approve. Andrew got a truly colourful bruised face and chipped teeth for his trouble. But the quest for fun was too important to all of us; Andrew especially and he was soon chatting up the girls once again. I had my obligatory holiday romance with a girl called Emily from Essex. Hardly Mediterranean or exotic for a first romance though. I do remember that she had the most enormous breasts which would wobble when she waved. I also think my lips needed resuscitating after the amount of exercise they were getting and she was very keen on trying to find my tonsils. I also admit, as late as it was I lost my virginity to Emily, lying on the beach on a rough cheap hotel towel in the pitch black. I swear I had sand in all orifices for days after. It was the most horrendous experience of my teenage years. I'd also made the huge mistake of seeking advice from our own Don Juan, Andrew, as he had had more sex with girls by the time he was eighteen than he had toes. I cannot repeat the advice he gave me as the mere thought of it makes me shudder. Put it this way it just wasn't an epic experience he claimed it to be.

Not long after we returned from Ibiza, George's mother was diagnosed with cancer, she was only 47. His mum was like a second mum to us all; she cooked us meals, put up with our noise; gave us a bed if required; was someone you could confide in and someone who truly loved people unconditionally. It was so unexpected that it was hard for us to take it all in. George of course was devastated. None of us had experienced anything like this before and suddenly the sad harsh reality of life had exposed itself. Shockingly it was only a few months after her diagnosis that she died but George and his family were able to stay with her until the end. Her death stunned us all and impacted on me in more ways than imaginable; hers would be the first funeral that all of us attended and it wasn't just his mum that died that day. It was the George we knew.

On the day of the funeral John, Harries and I met in the local pub, none of us had spoken to George since the day she died. Andrew of course had. If anyone could support him in his hour of need it was going to be him. George had two older sisters, who naturally babied him like sisters do, and had his father for support so we felt rather redundant. George was exceptionally close to his mother, something I never understood after being brought up by my mother and I felt nothing we could say or do would make him feel even the slightest bit better. Not that any of us really knew what to say.

I didn't know what to expect at a funeral apart from what I had seen in the movies. I was glad that the funeral was a small affair, it was kept that way despite the hordes of friends, neighbours and co-workers who wished to pay their respects. After a short service and a terribly moving tribute by George's father her body was laid to rest in a cemetery close to their home. George was the last to approach the coffin; he took a photo from his pocket and gently let it drop from his hand. He stood seemingly paralysed, eyes focused fiercely downwards. It was an agonising wait until his father stepped in to gently usher him away. Etched in my brain is picture of the four of us watching George struggling in his father's comforting arms, so reluctant to leave his mother's side. His two lovely sisters, usually so full of joy and humour clung onto each other for support. I had never been in so much pain with sadness. Tears had been free flowing from all of us since the start of the service and none of us even tried manfully to stop. We would all miss her and to this very day I still miss her, she was an incredible, genuine lady and the perfect mother. Andrew said his own goodbyes to her and before we had a chance to talk to him he was quietly taken back home by his parents. I never saw or heard from Andrew again. Harries would meet him once more but after that he completely disappeared from our lives.

George changed after his mother's death. The fun, funny, talkative guy had become more introspective and very rarely laughed. He postponed his place at university and practically became reclusive in his parents' home. When we met up a few months after her death he was unrecognisable in that everything about him was slower, his physicality even his speech. He cried horribly at her funeral and sadly he never really recovered from her loss. He moved to Los Angeles with his family a year later. When I last visited George he had a job in a music studio and seemed to be getting his life together but he wasn't the same. Being a grown up and suffering so much loss had crept up quickly on George, on all of us.

Our group, now adults rather than teenagers, went our separate ways finally putting away the joys of youth and entering the world of adulthood, to finally become a grownup. Harries became a stock broker in the City and John set up his own plastering business. Our trip to Ibiza was the parting gift of teenage friendship never to be repeated.

Again I digress. After my clear up, the decorators moved in and the room became nothing more than a spare room. The walls were white, the carpet changed and the furniture brand new. I can't believe they had that much faith in Sebastian not to transform the room to his liking; a clinical white is far from homely and in my opinion not terribly sensible given Sebastian's proclivities for decoration.

XV

Four long months had passed when Sebastian was released into my parents care, they naturally were anxious and scared at the prospect of Sebastian living at home but I think Sebastian's fears were far greater than theirs. He still perceived the world as a hostile place even though he was going home. He would also have the handicap of reduced vision and the expected stares and laughs from the public. The scarred eye was pretty frightening to look at as nothing aesthetic was performed on it. My father was all too ready to get his check book out if it could mean a more pleasing scar.

The day we picked him up he seemed non-committal about going home with us. He sat in his usual position on the floor with a somewhat confused expression on his face when my father entered the room. Sebastian's face was now fuller due to the effect of weight gain from medication and his beard had been finally shaved off. It wasn't just the physical that had changed but his whole manner. We found him to be more intrusive and without boundaries. My parents were shocked and appalled when he would only eat with his fingers. His doctor had forewarned us that he would get easily upset over relative minor things and night times were still the most distressing for him. There were still parts of his character that remained, he was still a gentle boy, he still had the childish giggle but sadly it was part of the psychosis as the response to the voices in his head. The voices of angels.

It was a brief goodbye to the ward staff and I made a particular effort to say thank you to Melanie. She was a godsend to me throughout all this. I hoped she wouldn't become too hardened to the ward and the job as many nurses often do. Once we were in the car he immediately began to giggle. It was hard to ignore in the beginning but over time we got used to it, of course others didn't. It created nervousness among other people but we knew it was harmless, that is unless he suffered another serious episode while un-medicated. I think the voices gave him some sort of comfort, sometimes the giggling would last for seconds, other times minutes.

The drive home was an interesting one. My father concentrated, rightly so, on the driving, never leaving his focus from the road. I sat in the back with Sebastian trying to continue bonding with a boy that was now almost alien to me. I remember just staring at him while he stared intently out of the window. I tried banal conversation to begin with but the response was either a shrug of the shoulders or nothing at all. I continued trying. "What do you want to do when we get home?" Once again no response either vocally or physically, there was no turn off the head in recognition when I spoke. "Do you want the window open? Dad can you open the window back here?" The window came down and Sebastian quickly backed off as if there was something unpleasant or scary going on outside.

It came out of nowhere, "I want a beer."

"A beer sounds good to me. Pub beer or home beer?"

"Just beer."

Our mother came out to greet us when we arrived, well I say greet but there wasn't much happy greeting visible in her stance or face. Her arms were crossed and no smile radiated from her face as her youngest child exited to car. It was like she was greeting a prospective lodger. It was so very sad to see and I hoped that Sebastian would be no wiser. I know that she loved him but just not in the way that a mother truly loved a child. This was the time that he really needed George's mum to show him that he was the most important thing to her. She was responsible once again for an almost man/child and at the beginning both my parents really struggled.

Once in his room, he stood for a few moments in the middle of the room taking in his new sparse surroundings. We hadn't painted over the ceiling so the cosmos still existed in his bedroom. He sat dejectedly on the bed and I could see how in his mind he was going to rearrange the furniture and dismantle the bed and who could blame him he; had a room that contained his whole, but largely unwell, life which had now become an exact replica of his hospital room, just not as filthy. He had a lot of adapting to do especially being now blind in one eye and I could sense that it was going to be an uphill struggle for him. I was going to stay until my parents were able to cope and Sebastian was well settled in his new environment. What I didn't plan for was how long this process was going to take. Susan had taken Cosmo to Cambridge and I envisaged seeing her only at the weekends so my love life was put on the back burner once again.

I was surprised though when I opened the spanking new wardrobe to put his minimalistic clothing in I found it full of new clothes, everything you could possibly wear was new in that wardrobe. My mother had been to Marks and Spencer and I'm sure bought the whole of the men's department. I do not believe however that it was an amazing turnaround of my mother's generosity but a flashing sign signalling him to change his clothes more often. Likewise in the bathroom, that only he used, were copious amounts of soap, toothpaste and deodorants.

As the time passed he became visibly anxious, the

unfamiliarity of the room became too much for him to take in. He began to pace in a small circle muttering to himself, it was like I was watching 'Rainman'. It was becoming frightening for him and for me as I tried hopelessly to find out what he wanted or what I could do to ease his anxiety.

"My bible; all my bibles."

"They're here." I showed him the shelf where I'd arranged all his books and just then I realised that where he was standing they were hidden from his line of sight. "There all here, in alphabetical order, in subject order just as you had them before. And look your universe is still there; you can still lie in bed and look at the stars." He stopped pacing and began reviewing my organisation of his books. He naturally rearranged things but I was quite pleased with myself that I kind of got it right. "What about that beer then?" He looked puzzled and replied "What beer?" With that I left him to it.

The screams that night were agonizing. He had had his medication just a couple of hours before but they were far from helping. I was first out of bed as my room was nearest to his and I found him huddled naked in the corner of his room. The bed had been dismantled and he was now sleeping on what was now a bare mattress on the floor. My mother and father stood at the door watching as their son rocked himself back and forth crying in absolute terror of something that we could not see or hear.

It took me by surprise my mother broke away from my father and was at my brother's side. He wasn't happy being touched but she was there with him and finally comforting him as a mother should. Deep down I knew she couldn't distance herself from him for much longer.

Although he physically balked at her attempts to hug him it was the first of many nights that my mother would just sit on his bed until he eventually fell asleep. It was like having a new-born baby in the house, the sleepless nights and the helplessness of not knowing what they want. It was always my mother who performed this duty; my father would continue his regime of bed at ten, up at six and then back home at eight. Sebastian was hard work and it did not take long before my mother began to look tired and old. Her unreasonable husband was still her unreasonable husband. At times I know my mother was close to breaking point, 24 hour care and stuck in the house with an 18 year old unable to look after himself would be exhausting for anyone.

A few months after his release, Susan moved down to Sussex to live with me. It would be a struggle financially and at first emotionally. She applied for a few jobs locally, the choice of course being limited and we knew any salary would not be anywhere as close to the one in Cambridge. She was also two months pregnant. I couldn't take in at first: I would be a father at 23, have a girlfriend more than a decade older than me, I had no experience of children and I didn't know whether I could cope. I always thought about having children but not in my early twenties and not before marriage. Susan was initially in a state of shock, as I'm sure a lot of women are when they discover that they are pregnant. She was worried, as was I, that we had only been together for a matter of months and we hardly knew each other. We did discuss the possibility of termination but neither of us really felt that that was truly the best option. We waited weeks before we told my parents and as you can imagine there was no banners or balloons at our impending arrival or enthusiasm about the prospect of them becoming grandparents. It was just another untenable situation.

As the months passed the situation with my parents and Sebastian began to improve and little by little he settled into a routine. He was able to leave the house, first accompanied by my mother; they would go to the park or a café and then finally he would go out alone. It was a worry of course but, ultimately, inevitable and for a couple of months it proved to be successful. He would appear for meals and then escape to his room or go out. My parents never asked where he went for fear of the answer. After then he would disappear all night and once home would just sleep all day like he was a vampire.

In those early months there was a small hiatus by my father who just couldn't deal with Sebastian anymore and my mother's constant attention to him. Two months after Seb had been at home my father left for work as normal but didn't return that night; he stayed away for three weeks. My parents owned a flat in Kensington that my father often stayed at if he was working late. My mother had enough to worry about; the least of her worries would be a jealous, unreasonable husband. He returned as if nothing had happened it was as if he had just been on holiday by himself but what could my mother do? She was a housewife and full time carer; my father's needs were becoming less and less important.

My father was entrusted with the task of accompanying Seb to any doctor's appointments; now a private psychiatrist from the Priory which was close by. He made it crystal clear what he wanted from the doctor and on the first appointment raised the serious problem of the screaming at night. Sebastian was sleeping for around three to four hours maximum a night. He duly prescribed a stronger sedative and increased his anti-psychotics. For a while these seemed to work but within a few weeks he was back to the same. My parents would be awoken by the screams, head to his bedroom, find him huddled on the floor wrapped in a blanket fraught with anxiety. The doctor told them that they just had to deal with it the best they could as he was reluctant to increase the dosage above the designated maximum dose. They were given stronger sedation for emergency purposes only. So the sleepless nights continued. To their credit, as the weeks passed by, my parents seemed to be adapting; my father became in charge of his personal grooming and bathing and my mother everything else. He also cut down his hours of work, as he was approaching sixty and was looking then at retirement. Despite the great strain and stressful environment they were coping much better than I had envisaged they would but the gap between my parents relationship was visibly wider. I thought he might leave her again and he did, but only for a few nights in town, when he prepared for a difficult case.

So as it was things in the Bradbury household were running, not exactly smoothly but as best as it could be. Sebastian was willingly taking his medication under the auspicious of both my mother and father and when his anxiety would reduce him into mammoth tears, if he stayed in that is, my mother would still sit with him for however long it took. On two occasions when he had a really bad night my father would take in his comfy chair and stay all night too. He wasn't happy about it but, to be perfectly honest, I didn't care less about his discomfort or unhappiness.

As for me, I was finally coming out of the emotional abyss that started with Sebastian's admission but I'd also gained a live-in pregnant girlfriend. I can't say that everything was rosy when she moved in, as we'd barely spent a full weekend together, and there were, I confess, more than a few petty arguments; that I'm sure is no different from any other relationship. Susan had stocked piled the baby books and got busy choosing colour schemes for the baby's room. I confess I feigned interest in many of the baby decisions illustrating to me how high up in the list of priorities our imminent arrival was.

At that time the uncertainness and my insecurity plagued heavily in our relationship. Susan, being an older mother, had more stresses and strains from that of younger mothers and the chances of the baby being born with an abnormality were, in Susan's case, high. She refused point blank to abort when we were advised of this but I knew she felt that this may be one of her last chances to have a child when she was still young enough to enjoy it. She balked at the idea of being nearly forty or older as a first time mum. As for me I was indifferent, harsh as though it may sound.

Macie was a tower of strength through the final stages of her pregnancy; she travelled from Cambridge whenever Susan needed her. My parents, as I expected, kept a wide berth, especially my mother as she always told me that she couldn't leave Sebastian in order to visit and it was inconceivable that she would drive him down to us. My father was left with him solely only on the rarest of occasions. I visited every few weeks and would take him to the pub or for a coffee. His scarred face of course was stared at but he didn't seem to take much notice. I noticed; and on the first few occasions got quite angry and upset about it. After time the pub regulars welcomed us in and no questions were ever asked. The only major problem for Seb in the beginning with his disability was the judging of space and unexpected obstacles either on the pavements or in the places we went. He did trip quite spectacularly in a cafe when a woman dumped her very large handbag directly outside his field of vision. She was apoplectic with apologies but later Sebastian told me she was very cute and was quite happy to trip over anything of hers. The sexual side of Sebastian came out more overtly in Italy. There is always a perception that schizophrenics don't have sexual urges or feelings, they couldn't be more wrong.

Susan gave birth to a boy at our home and we named him Aaron, after Susan's father. He was a very small baby but a healthy one. Susan was in heaven; her world was centred purely on him. Rather than increasing the visible gap that had existed between us it made our bond stronger. When I saw my son, I finally became a grown man and a father. We both doted on Aaron; the sleepless nights were equally shared. The numerous times I had sat with Sebastian had prepared me for the tiredness and irritability. Sometimes, when it was warm outside, we would sit on the terrace and listen to the sea; just appreciating the luxury of having our home and our family. I was finally content.

XVI

One year later. We stood before the clerk at the check in desk at Heathrow, boarding for Florence. I was nervous yet excited, I hadn't had a holiday for over two years and I'd never been just with Sebastian. He stood beside me fidgeting. Despite all the family's efforts he still looked badly dressed and unkempt although the Jesus beard and hair look had long since gone. The desk clerk, I could clearly see, was uncomfortable with him and shifted nervously in her seat. His passport photo naturally was quite different to his look as the scarring on his eye and cheekbones were quite apparent. It was an error on our part not to renew his documents so I did expect to be questioned about it. Surprisingly we weren't.

"Where do you wish to be seated Sir?"

Sebastian put both hands on the desk, "Not near the front, not near the back but not in the middle as the plane may crash and break in two." Tears then started and I didn't know if it was because he didn't want to get on the plane or because he just didn't want to go on holiday at all. "Not this airline." It wasn't British Airways put it that way.

"Sir, do you wish to continue to check in?"

I looked at Sebastian; it was an unequivocal 'no'. I led him away from the desk under the staring eyes of the whole queue. His eyes said everything to me so I grabbed the bags and made for the exit. "We can go another day, it doesn't matter. Let's just go home." We were at my parents an hour later and needless to say they were not surprised to see us. I read, 'told you so' on my father's face. Sebastian as soon as we arrived ran up to his room closely followed by my mother.

Two weeks later we tried again, this time on a British Airways flight which was far more expensive of course.

My father did cough up the money for the plane tickets this time. Sebastian believed that the more quality the carrier the better quality the plane. Cheap seats equals cheap plane was his line of thinking. Cheap planes he said crash more. I didn't care who we flew with but it caused great anxiety and apprehension for him and his impenetrable wall of reasoning went up if he felt threatened.

That morning he had had a scare which I had hoped would not interfere with the rest of the day. Seb had been in his room, doing God knows what, when he saw a face suddenly appearing in the window, it was the window cleaner. According to my mother Seb was hysterical and believed he was being spied on and 'they' were coming to get him. It didn't help matters when the cleaner knocked on the window to ask him to shut one of them. My mother heard the commotion, ran upstairs and found Seb in the corner of his room, eyes tightly closed screaming. I think the poor window cleaner was more shocked than Sebastian and my parents did not expect his services in the future. Seb still lived in that bubble of fear but it was manageable for us to deal with. He was still very much awake at night but the screaming had thankfully reduced considerably. I knew it would be different on holiday and there would just be me but I felt I could cope. Susan was vehemently against the idea and repeatedly warned me of the problem if he needed hospital attention. I knew the risk and was prepared to accept it.

So there we were again, we had also managed to fast track a new passport for Sebastian. Everything was going fine until the barrage of questions about the luggage. He replied to the question of anyone packing your case other than yourself with 'I'm always helped. God helps me and shows me the way. Clothes are not a necessity as they cloak the real person inside. Benjamin also helps me and I don't know what is in there. I have no need for material things.' Well that was enough for the desk clerk and her supervisor. Sebastian's illness prevented his ability to interpret and respond appropriately in response to questioning. It's just one of the pernicious aspects of schizophrenia that continually plagued him.

I attempted to explain the situation and that sometimes basic tasks had to be completed by others, such as packing, and that he had schizophrenia. It seemed the word schizophrenic was enough and after a long discussion the officials were not prepared to allow any leeway by letting us on the aircraft. They deemed him too much of a possible disturbance to others on the flight and we were consequently not allowed to fly. To be honest I could see it happening and wasn't surprised or even angry at their response. It didn't even cross my mind to ask about a refund. It wasn't contestable that his behaviour could be disturbing and I naively thought that that could be concealed on an aircraft with him sitting close beside me. I was disappointed of course but if we couldn't fly we would drive.

I decided that we would take the Eurostar to Paris and I would hire a car from there. It wasn't the best plan but it was all I had. The journey to St Pancras was stressful enough. The stares and faces of fear and pity as we stepped out the taxi at the station were upsetting to me but Seb didn't seem to notice. At least once I heard 'poor bastard' uttered and I was unsure whether they were talking about him or me. The first seats available were not seated together, a situation which would be untenable so we had to wait and wait and wait. It was 5pm when we eventually boarded a train. Both of us were tired and irritable but I was proud of Sebastian that he was able to stay calm and patient throughout the mammoth wait.

I managed to get a little sleep but really wanted to stay awake to keep an eye on Sebastian. Seated opposite when we boarded was a young woman with a small child. I could clearly see, as we sat down, the young woman's uneasiness when she immediately grabbed her child, who was quite happily sitting on the chair playing with a toy car, and onto her lap. I made a point of saying hello, both in French and English, and she gave a meek smile. It didn't help that Sebastian was giggling to himself. I must have dropped off not long after we left the station. When I woke I found the woman and child had been replaced by two businessman. I was under no illusion as to what had happened. I acknowledged them and turned to Seb who was thankfully asleep. Once we had arrived in France I took this time to ring Susan and she was well and truly pissed at me. I took the abuse and did my best to calm the situation. I explained our predicament to her and once again explained that I was going to do as I promised and take Sebastian to Florence. She reluctantly conceded defeat after a few minutes and I promised I'd be extra careful and phone her daily.

I woke Sebastian about 10 minutes before we arrived at Gare du Nord. It was too late to hire a car that night so I checked us into a small hotel near the station. It was quite pricey but for one night the expense I thought would be minimal. My primary goal was to get us food and give Sebastian his meds. Both were dealt with within 10 minutes. I decided on room service to save our energy, time and allow for an early night. Once in the room though we encountered a problem.

"The bed is strange."

"I know but it's just for one night." The only room available was a double room and he'd have to share with me and he was far from happy. "You'll be right next to me, nothing is going to happen to you, and it's just one night."

"NO! I'm not sleeping there; I've got a strange feeling. I'm not sleeping there."

"How about I put a blanket on the floor, would you be happy with that?" He nodded so I threw a couple of spare blankets from the wardrobe on the floor. After we ate I organised our money situation, I'd need more cash for definite. I had two credit cards, one for emergencies and one for general use, which would gradually become indistinguishable from each other. We hadn't been away a day and the costs were slowly piling up especially from the cost of the train tickets. Sebastian was sound asleep when I eventually put the light out.

As soon as we had had breakfast we went straight to Avis to hire a car, another huge expense and I chose the most basic small car without Sat Nav. I'd bought a copy of the AA guide to European roads before we left London. Map reading was not my skill but it was Sebastian's. People often underestimate the capability of the mentally ill but vast numbers of affected people have many expert skills still available to them, artists like Van Gogh, poets such as Sylvia Plath and the many actors who work with depression or bipolar disorder. So, Sebastian quite easily led us onto a major road heading out of Paris towards the town of Reims where we would spend the night. I estimated that it would take around 22 hours to drive to Italy; this route would take us through Switzerland. My driving skill and my need to take frequent breaks would seriously affect that estimated time but it gave us a chance to see more of Europe and hopefully keep me a safer driver.

The route to Reims was monotonous as it was a bland road through bland countryside; it was similar to the M1 in England. Sebastian slept all the way to Reims. Reims had been labelled as one of the main 'gastronomic centres in France' and was famous for its wine and champagne. I had to keep a clear head throughout this trip so the alcoholic delights that were so tempting had to be put on hold. The easiest and most convenient place to stay was in the Holiday Inn, with a blockbusting rate of 2 Stars. We certainly did not need luxury, just a shower and a comfy bed.

Sebastian was still tired and fell asleep on a rather shoddy two-man sofa not long after we checked in. Not feeling tired myself, I wrote him a note saying I'd gone out for an hour and that he was to stay in the room. I didn't stray very far at all as next to the hotel was a small café. I plonked myself down in a fairly comfy chair taking in the rays of the glorious sunshine. I must have sat there in my own world for a little more than an hour and had drunk at least three coffees, one of which was an eye popping espresso.

When I returned to the room Sebastian was pacing frantically up and down muttering to himself and covering his ears with his hands. "Hey, hey what's up?" I took away his hands from his ears, "Shh, what's wrong? Tell me what's wrong. Just be calm Seb, come on calm down. Shh now, you're all right."

"You left me, you left me."

"Fuck", it didn't even cross my mind that I couldn't leave him alone. He was going out all the time at home and he was left alone for a couple of hours on a few occasions without a problem. I should have known that an unfamiliar place would cause him anxiety. How could I have been so stupid? I left him in a strange hotel in a foreign country and thought nothing of it. I was going to have to be a lot more savvy that that for the rest of our trip. He continued to pace for a good ten minutes or so before he gradually stopped. The occasional muttering didn't stop but he grew a lot calmer. He had been prescribed some sedatives which would calm him but I didn't want him to be half comatose for the rest of the day, I vowed I wouldn't use them on this trip unless the situation really called for it. "I'm sorry. I won't leave you again. We'll do everything together okay. I promise."

"You promise?"

"Yeah, I promise. Shall we go out and see the town; see what France has to offer?" My French added up to the GCSE I took 6 years ago. I knew basic conversational French, the ordering of food or the asking for directions but anything more than that was completely alien to me. Our first visit was to the Musee de Beaux Arts, which turned out to have an impressive collection of impressionist paintings. Thanks to Sebastian's patience we were able to spend a couple of hours wandering the corridors and pausing at our favourite pieces. At various times we experienced a crowd but thankfully these were rare. Seb was less than enthusiastic when we tried to get a drink in the café. The wait was too long even for me.

On our walk back to the hotel we stopped at the Cathedral, a Roman Catholic church. I was wary of Sebastian's behaviour at the last church so I stayed close to him, ready to eject him from there if necessary. I allowed him to light a candle and say a small prayer.

He didn't tell me whom he prayed for, I just felt guilty as a lapsed Catholic of just being in there. All the religious fervour of the last year left a bad taste in my mouth and made me despise that bloody religion. It didn't however stop me from enjoying the beauty and intricacies of the art itself.

Later we had dinner in a small quiet restaurant near the hotel. Conversation turned into a one man show on my side. He nodded or shook his head to questions but very rarely gave a long response. He remained very quiet when I asked how living with our parents was and after a long pause replied, "Okay". It was obvious to me that he disliked it but there was no other option open to us. When he reached 21 he could be sent to a group home but that idea just left me cold. If it wasn't for Aaron I'd have him living with Susan and me.

Back at the hotel I took a much needed shower as the heat outside was still stifling and the air conditioning unit in the room was crap. I could smell the sweat on Sebastian so I had the daunting time consuming task of getting him to shower also. He still had a strong aversion to water but perseverance usually paid off. His answer usually in regards to showering was that as he was Jesus it was he who did the anointing in water and my claim that Jesus was baptized in the River Jordan by John the Baptist always seemed to be ignored. After the usual techniques not working, the only answer was to physically push him under the stream of water but you had to get him in the bathroom first. That part, often tricky, was quite easy; he just followed me in there and removed his clothes as I chatted to him. I turned on the shower pulled him towards me, pushed him under the water and then ducked quickly out the way. My mother used this technique quite often but it did make a huge mess on the floor and risked her being soaked from head to foot. On at least two occasions he refused to remove his clothes so she just had to let him keep them on. Once under the water he seemed not to be too bothered about it.

Sebastian slept on the floor as usual; as it was so warm I didn't worry too much about him not wanting any blankets. I must have nodded off only minutes after my head hit the pillow but something had been praying on my conscience as I woke with a start around 3 a.m. Then it hit me, I hadn't given Seb his meds. I could see his silhouette by the window, he was sitting perfectly still. I turned on the light; the room looked like we had just been burgled. The drawers had been removed from the chest, the contents of the wardrobe were now on the floor and the suitcases emptied. Although very serene and still he obviously had been quite agitated and had probably been awake all this time. I was furious with myself, the only thing that had to be strictly followed on this trip was his medication regime and I had fucked up big time. I was unsure now whether to give him his dose from last night or his morning meds. The simplest solution was the one I was trying to avoid; the sedation. He'd be able to get at least four hours sleep if he took them now and so would I. He compliantly took the pills and lay down on the floor at the foot of the bed. He always took pills without water, something I could never do; I tried it once and they got stuck in my throat and I felt like I was coughing up fur balls all day. He fell asleep 20 long minutes later and I was back in bed and of course couldn't bloody get to sleep. I read the road map hoping that it was send me off.

XVII

I woke at 10am Sebastian was still asleep. I returned the room to its former state and sorted out a change of clothes for Seb and what we would need for the journey. I was keen to get going; it would still be hours driving to get to Zurich. The petrol was costing a small fortune.

The surrounding countryside was similar to that seen on the motorways of Britain. Pretty in some parts but incredibly dull for the most part. The roads were fairly clear of traffic so my temper thankfully never frayed at the bad driving skills of others or waiting in any queues. Our conversation was divided into three parts: no conversation, a little conversation or rambling, often delusional, conversation. Luckily this combination worked for me just fine. Due to my calculations we would be in Zurich in around six hours. We'd stop for lunch and I hoped to arrive in Zurich early afternoon. We would stay there overnight as I was not terribly keen on driving at night particularly on the wrong side of the road.

"Are you a good driver Ben?

"I hope so. Am I? We'll be in trouble if I'm not won't we?"

"You got a speeding ticket."

"Yes and I'm very contrite about it. It was just one of those things, you're all by yourself, the road is clear in front of you and you're just enjoying the drive and somehow the speed just creeps up on you. It must have been the funky George Michael track I was listening to, it made me drive faster."

"Well he isn't a good driver."

"No you're sure as hell right there, he was stoned mostly though, and that's bound to impair your judgement driving. He's a great songwriter though!"

"Do you smoke weed?"

"No."

"You do don't you? I remember Mum caught you and John smoking in the shed."

"That was a normal cigarette and Dad gave me a good slap behind the legs for it. The weed came later."

"What's it like?"

"Depends on the person really, I passed out and threw up on my first puff. It's not good Sebastian, much overrated. Why did you ask if I'm a good driver? Do you feel nervous with me driving?"

"Just thinking about methods of transport, none of them are safe."

"We could always swap to bicycles or horses. Do you remember Percy? We would have had to stop every ten minutes for a food break." Sebastian remained silent for a while after that but when I looked at my watch he suddenly came to life again.

"Time doesn't exist, Benjamin. It is a manmade concept; hours, minutes, seconds do not exist. Watches and clocks were merely inventions indicating periods of transition. If you do look at time, as most humans see it, the shortest 'time' is an attosecond which is 10 to the power of minus 18. Stars have the more measureable time, as it were, as it's the time relative to a distant star that is not solar time. Clocks merely measure the movement of the hands and a physical measurement but the concept of astronomical time and the length of time are way different. Clocks mean nothing to me because they are programmed. They are there to create order - 5hrs, 3hrs they just doesn't exist."

"So how do you account for the difference; being in one place and then in another and the period that lapsed?"

"Because there are other dimensions; overlapping in multi-dimensional universes. For humans we think that time is linear and continuous but it's not. There are multiple experiences overlapping and create an illusion of change."

"Can you just repeat that; so I can actually understand what you've just said?"

"It's easy: time does not exist. Do you wish Susan was here?"

"Why do you say that? No it's nice just the two of us. Susan has to look after Aaron. I don't think an eight month old baby can really appreciate art."

Sebastian seemed to be responding less to the voices in head; but I was so focused on driving that he could have been whispering the Lord's Prayer and not have noticed. Our onward journey would take a few hours but he seemed calmer and even seemed to be enjoying the views as we drove by. I came off the main road at lunchtime for a most welcome pee break. I had no idea of the beauty of the backroads of France, never really fancied going to France period. The freedom of driving was becoming something I really began to enjoy. We stopped when we wanted or when I thought I needed to attend more to Sebastian. I drove through the picturesque Swiss border and on to Zurich. Due to my poor map reading skills when Sebastian was sleeping I navigated way off course but I confess I was really enjoying the drive anyway. After a few pit stops along the way we arrived in Zurich early evening. Sebastian was a bit cranky initially but I ignored it for the most part.

My choice of hotel put me in the dog house however. We were checked in by a rather sour overweight frau with a moustache some men only dream of. The room stank of smoke but it didn't really bother me that much and was directly above a bar. After Sebastian had his meds and settled on the floor I lay on the bed trying to relax. The noise from the now busy bar below sounded like a flock of flamingos. On a trip to the zoo years ago I came to the conclusion that flamingos make an incredible muffled noise similar to that of people talking. I remained awake for such a long period of time I wondered whether to go down and have a beer myself. The disco music started around midnight and Sebastian woke up and immediately covered his ears with his hands. He wouldn't go back to sleep unless I stayed beside him. I had no choice but to watch him try and sleep with his ears covered over. The bed was creaky and so uncomfortable that I slept in the chair and the bathroom was a disaster waiting to happen. The paint and wall paper were peeling; the hot water tap was completely missing from the bath and there hung one solitary lightbulb from the ceiling, I'm sure there was mould mutating in there as well. It looked like a crime scene. There was no way Seb would ever have a bath or shower in there and quite frankly neither would I. I wouldn't be able to see him let alone supervise him. I finally dropped off around 3 and woke around 9 am. Surprisingly I felt quite refreshed, I sprung out the chair but something was missing. Seb wasn't on the floor. He wasn't in the bathroom either. I swore so loudly that they could have heard me in London. Panic is a word that just doesn't cover it. I put my shorts on so quickly that I lost my balance and then legged it out the door. I was terrified; terrified that he had wandered into town and I'd have to phone for the police.

I ran down two, could have been three, steps at a time into the reception area, a panic attack about to erupt. Then I saw him. He was seated outside the hotel on the steps, arms hugging his legs. I was angry but relieved.

"Why the hell did you leave the room? I nearly had a heart attack."

"It was too noisy; you were asleep so I came out here."

"How long have you been here?"

"I dunno; it was dark."

I grabbed him underneath his arm pit and pulled him up. I was probably rougher and angrier than I could have been. "For fuck sake don't wander off again. You stay with me." He didn't seem to be listening to anyone, he was off in his own little Sebastian world, giggling and mumbling to himself. I took him back to the room, threw a new pair of shorts and a t shirt at him and gave him his meds. Once he was organised and, more importantly, medicated I tidied myself up and then sat on the bed counting our remaining Euros. The budget was now no budget at all but just expense. My original figure was way off, Switzerland was a bloody expensive country, and I was near reaching the limit on one of the credit cards. The train and the petrol had nearly maxed it out. If we kept going as we were I'd have to ring my father to wire some money. I made the decision over breakfast that we would spend another night here. I needed the break from driving and Sebastian needed at least one night of uninterrupted sleep. We would of course move to a different hotel.

As cost was by now getting ludicrously immaterial I found a reasonable hotel in the old part of town; it was small and was located on a very quiet street. When the time was right I rang my father to ask him to wire me some money, until then MasterCard was my best friend. Susan would quite literally kill me. Our finances were not good when she moved in and I had to take extra article writing jobs for an amateur painters' publication. It pained me to do so but it paid a bill every month.

Apart from being ridiculously expensive, Zurich had an incredible architectural and cultural heritage. The opera house was stunningly beautiful. Sebastian wasn't particularly keen but followed me around uncomplaining nonetheless. We visited the modern art gallery to satisfy his art tastes and saw some Andy Warhol, Picasso's and one of Sebastian's favourite paintings by Salvador Dali: 'The Persistence Of Memory', the painting well known for the elongated time pieces. It fitted in so well with his fascination with Dali and with his theory of the nonexistence of time. These visits took up most of the day and I was somewhat thankful when Sebastian confessed to being tired and asked that we return to the hotel. On our way back though we saw a sign for the Urania Observatory and Seb was keen to stop and I was keen for a drink. We paused at the café before going in and were subject to uncomfortable stares as Sebastian ate with just his fingers. Every once in a while he would pick up a fork if asked but I got tired of asking. It wasn't just the finger technique drawing the stares but the increased giggling and mumbling. It always seemed louder and worse in public despite my attempts to keep his mind occupied. The gawping public just had to deal with its own prejudices. I must confess though his Jesus look was creeping back as he had three days of stubble stuck to his chin.

He was completely spellbound by the observatory and its magnificent telescope which according to him was a masterpiece in technology. There were three guided tours: the moon, the solar system and interstellar clouds (whatever they were) and other galaxies. He wanted to see all three and the expression on his face as he marvelled in the vast outer space was worth the admission alone. After many, many months of misery I saw him smile, a genuine smile. We spent at least three hours lost in the cosmos as Sebastian explained in fine detail mind-blowing facts and figures. If it wasn't for his blunting of emotions, which schizophrenia carries, I would have gone as far as to say that he was happy. Perversely I felt kind of sad that this moment of happiness would last only for a few minutes or even just a few hours before he would return to his normal state. As we stepped out into the bright sunlight I could see his face return to its set position. Despite our teething troubles so far I was beginning to really enjoy the journey.

Sebastian was tired, as was I, from all the walking and I wanted to be able to enjoy a relaxing bath and phone Susan uninterrupted. Macie was staying with her for a few days and doted on Aaron as if he were her own grandchild. Her son Tom had never wanted children and had no inclination to join Elton John and David Furnish in the 'two gay parents' stake. I reassured Susan that everything was fine and we were having a good time. I could tell by the tone of her voice that she was sceptical. My father was positive it would be disastrous.

Sebastian's bathing process took a lot less time as he just wanted to go to bed as quickly as he could and was willing to stand under the shower, literally just standing stock still and letting the water spill over him. As long as his sweaty body hit some kind of water I'd didn't really care. I took to throwing his old clothes in the bin so he wouldn't wear them again. Even if I put them in the car they would manage to wrangle themselves back on his body. I ordered room service; switched on the television and watched some football on Eurosport and settled down for the night.

I was awakened sometime later to a knocking sound. Thinking it was the door I leapt out of bed, tripped over my shoes, flicking on the light as I passed and opened the door. No-one but I could still hear it. I turned back to bed and found the source of the noise. Sebastian was knocking on the bathroom walls.

"What you doing Seb?"

"Checking."

"Checking for what?"

"Things."

"There is nothing in those walls apart from plaster. Stop knocking and go to sleep. The neighbours will complain. Come away from there."

"Shh; you can hear them. Don't talk too loud otherwise they'll get angry."

"Please Sebastian, just go to bed, they'll be still there in the morning and if they are it doesn't matter as we'll be leaving anyway. I'm going back to bed." I got back in bed, arranged my pillow to muffle any sound and tried to shut out Seb. I woke up with a start, I don't know how long after I'd fallen asleep, it was my reoccurring dream but it wasn't so nearly as disturbing now. I felt a presence beside me so I turned over and curled up beside me asleep was Sebastian.

XVIII

Milan was the next stop on our journey; we would finally be in Italy. I let Sebastian sleep; taking the time to relax in the quiet sitting on the balcony. The sun was following us around providing me with nature's natural vitamins. It would be a five hour journey to Milan via the back roads. Sebastian said very little in the car and I thought he seemed a little 'off'. After lunch in a quaint little café, he curled up on the backseat and slept. His nocturnal activities were interrupting sleep for the both of us. As much as I was enjoying the quiet it did leave me with a sense of uneasiness. He woke when we crossed the border into Italy.

"Are we there?"

"Just crossing into Italy, it's only an hour or so from here. You have been sleeping a lot, are you okay?"

"Why shouldn't I be?"

"I'm just asking, no problem about it. Are you having a good time?"

"It's alright."

"Just alright? You're not happy with my riveting personality and incredible language and driving skill then?" He looked at me with suspicion. "Last night, who exactly are 'they' in the walls?"

"The People. They listen to everything we say and watch everything we do. They sometimes talk to me and they frighten me sometimes but you do have to obey them."

"You're safe with me."

"Maybe."

As we drew nearer, the scenery seemed to change its whole personality. The winding roads took us through the magnificent hills, through small towns, across pretty bridges and streams. It was the Italy I knew existed. On a few occasions we parked the car and took a walk.

In the small village of Cherno there was a beautiful small church with a stunning stained glass window. Sebastian wanted to enter but I was still concerned about his behaviour since we set off. I could have been cautious but I just thought what the hell; what could he do that he hasn't done already.

Directly ahead on entering was another stained glass window above the altar; it depicted the crucifixion. I felt humbled; the lack of my religious fervour was creeping up too quickly upon me. Sebastian immediately made the sign of the cross and fell upon his knees in prayer which seemed a little Hollywood movie to me. Two elderly women came in clutching their rosaries. They seated themselves in a pew near the front and raised their heads to the statue of Christ, which was almost suspended from the rafters. I parked my arse on a pew at the back and waited for Sebastian to finish his religious ablutions.

The town of Lucca was a gem in the Italian countryside. It was ringed by huge walls and was situated on the River Serchio. Susan would have loved Lucca; it had cobbled streets, quaint cafes and boutique shops. The only problem was parking and the only place I could manage safely and successfully was outside the walls. Italians park wherever they want regardless of consequences or inconvenience. The centre of London was a piece of cake compared to here. Italians seemed to drive with blindfolds on.

The Basilica di San Frediano had a beautiful mosaic frontage, with incredible detail. I stood outside marvelling in its splendour when interrupting the idyllic moment were shouts of "Scosta! Scosta!" translated meant 'go away'. They could only have been talking about Sebastian who had gone in a few minutes before.

I darted into the church and saw Sebastian, bare-chested in front of the altar, posing as Christ on the cross.

"Sebastian!" An elderly man came to the aid of the two women who were shouting and cried "Si prega di lascioure," at me. I nodded furiously at his request to move Sebastian out of the church. I grabbed the t shirt off the floor, threw my arm around his waist and dragged him out.

"I need to stay to speak to God."

"We've been asked to leave; you can speak to God later. Put your t-shirt on."

"He was going to speak to me Benjamin."

"He'll have to wait I'm afraid. We need to get going." I was loathe to get into an argument so I dropped the subject as soon as I could. Sebastian seemed like he was sulking. I didn't care as long as he followed on behind. I was so comfortable with him now that his odd eccentricities were just that and his 'God' talks didn't bother me either. It was far easier for us to adapt to him than he to us. Ten minutes after trailing behind me he was back beside me.

The temperature was soaring, our pasty skin was beginning to burn and my feet were beginning to toast on the cobbled streets. I don't recommend flip flops in 90 degree heat. We stayed in Lucca for a splendid lunch, so splendid in fact that Sebastian even used a fork! He was far more relaxed as we journeyed on; there were a few instances of prolonged giggling but nothing to scare the horses.

"What will we see in Florence?"

"There's the Uffizi gallery. Botticelli, Michelangelo, Da Vinci, Giotto and there's the modern art museum too. We can go where ever we want."

"Did you know that Venus shown in Botticelli was his muse and was a married woman who died years before he did? And that he was buried underneath her tombstone. He died from unrequited love."

"No I didn't know that."

"Do you think it exists?"

"What?"

"Real love. You're not married?"

This question came from left field and I spluttered a bit before I answered, "We have no wish to be married. It doesn't mean I that don't love her."

"You do love her then?"

"Of course, why are you asking?"

"You sometimes just look miserable together."

"Do we? I love Susan and I love Aaron."

"She's nearly Mum's age."

I had to laugh; she was in fact old enough to be his mother, "It's a question of compatibility not age. We love each other and we're happy, that's all that matters to us." I got the feeling from his line of questioning that he wanted to confide in me or ask me something.

"Sarah."

"Sarah?"

"On the ward."

"Ah, that Sarah. She was a nice girl, pretty."

"I asked her out."

"And she said no?"

"She said maybe."

"Maybe wasn't enough was it?"

"No."

"You'll find another Sarah, an even nicer one." He looked sad and disappointed. It certainly seemed that little brother was growing into a more sexual being with feelings deeper than we had thought. Rejection is difficult for everyone but it would be far more of an uphill struggle for a schizophrenic like Sebastian. There would be no Hollywood romance for him. "Being rejected by a girl is a natural part of being a man."

"What about Mum and Dad?"

"What about them?"

"They are miserable. Dad yells at Mum, sometimes she yells back."

"After 25 years of marriage, they've earnt the right to be a little pissed with each other."

"It's because of me isn't it?"

Yes, yes it was I wanted to say but I couldn't say that to him. They were managing fine, in their own way, before his illness. After illness my mother lived in pure stress and tiredness and my father just sat back and let her cope and suffer with it all. The softer elements of my mother's personality came out after his return home from hospital but so did her anger. It was suggested by his doctor that they employ a private nurse during the day to allow my mother some respite but that suggestion went down like a lead balloon with my father. He never gave a reason either; I thought it was perhaps due to the fact that he was too embarrassed to show that they could not cope and his pride got in the way.

"Mum and Dad are just fine, with us and without us. You need not worry."

"Susan looks at me funny."

"Funny? How?"

"She scares me sometimes; her eyes."

Susan's eyes were bright green, quite heavenly to look at. "She loves you, she wouldn't harm you. She's stayed with you several times when Mum was out with me when we visit; I thought you have good times." All this evil eye business was completely new and a surprise to me.

"She's part of the 'People' Ben; the people in the walls; she has been sent out to spy on me."

"That is just ridiculous; I'm still here aren't I; I haven't been taken away? I wouldn't be here talking to you now would I? She's not one of them and she cares about you greatly. You like Aaron and being an uncle don't you?" Sebastian was incredibly gentle with the baby and if he cried he would gently rock him or hand him back to one of us. We had no problems with him handling our son. My mother remained indifferent to Susan and to Aaron; she had no interest in becoming a grandmother, it was difficult enough task being a second time mother. Any sort of retirement for my parents flew straight out the window, at least for a few more years.

"Did you know that the crater of Mars looks the same as the sand dunes in the Sahara desert and that there are billions of tiny microorganisms magnified by 1,000? They are all around us, floating in space and they fall on us like rain on the entire earth. We breathe them in and they are all around us. They enter your body and will take over your soul. It's inevitable. If we are lucky we will be saved and we will become angels. It's just a matter of time; none of us are truly safe."

"It's not happened yet has it? If they are everywhere; in you and me I don't feel any different."

"They are white light."

"What are?"

"Angels."

"If we are taken where do we go?"

"Hell of course; the fiery furnace; Satan's sofa. I think Susan is infected but she might be able to be saved."

"I'd like that."

"If it is written in the stars then it will take place. I pray for her sometimes and if I can I will help her Benjamin."

"Well that's good, thank you."

He stopped talking and turned around on the front seat to face the back. I didn't think to check his seatbelt was on. "Seatbelt Sebastian. Put it on." He compliantly did so and turned his attention out the side window. For the next hour or so he remained silent. I had refrained from switching on the radio as certain types of music can cause him distress. Thumping bass music made him very agitated. Classical music, often used as therapy, caused no obvious reaction and so my parents would play it frequently at home. Hours and hours of Vivaldi didn't appeal to me.

The temperature outside was cripplingly high and inside the car it was oppressive. The air conditioning had packed in just before we reached Switzerland and Sebastian didn't want the windows open. He didn't like the feel of the air on his face but I would have stood quite happily in a wind tunnel. I was melting so much that you could have fried an egg on my forehead. We were continuing to travel off map so we meandered through the tranquil back roads and through the tiny villages and towns, stopping occasionally to take a walk or stop for food. Despite his usual proclivities, the mumbling and giggling Sebastian seemed considerably relaxed. As long as we stuck to our routine he was fine, deviation was the problem and I felt proud of him that he was managing this trip so well so far.

XIX

We finally arrived in Florence, my favourite city in Italy. I had been there several times before with Sophia. I thought it may feel a bit strange emotionally coming here without her but it was not an emotion that actually surfaced. The next seven days would be spent here and I was revelling in the atmosphere as we drove into the city centre. Florence is a maze of one way streets and has the greatest population of erratic drivers I'd ever witnessed. I spent the first 15 minutes terrified before I took to driving a little less British. It was quite liberating beeping my horn furiously and shouting obscenities within the confines of the car. Florence may not have the delicate filigree of Venice or the romantic baroque of Rome but for me it was heaven.

I threw caution to the wind financially and checked us into a small hotel in the Piazza del Pescue, just behind the Pont Vecchio. It was more than I had, loosely, budgeted for but I thought we deserved it after my terrible choices on route. It had a lovely roof top garden and a secluded swimming pool. Our room, small but comfortable also had a balcony with a splendid view across the city. The first thing I wanted to do was to get out of the heat and just thought of my foot initially touching the water of the cool pool was exciting. The dilemma was what to do with Sebastian, there was no way he would go swimming or even dip his big toe in the water so it was a great surprise when he said he would accompany me down there but would stay well away from the water. We had both learn to swim at school; I was crap but, if push came to shove and I was out of my depth, I'd fight to the bitter end even swimming doggy paddle to survive in!

He didn't seem to mind the suggestion of sitting outside and followed me obediently down to the pool and found himself a space to sit down Buddha style and watch me.

"The Romans invented the swimming pool Benjamin and the largest is in Chile; its 115ft deep, is 1,000 yards long and eats up 66 million gallons of water. It has billions of microorganisms of course. You would die if you ran out of puff in the middle."

"Yes, thank you for that and I know I'm not the greatest swimmer but this pool is less than 20 feet and I'm hardly going to be chosen for the Olympics." I ensured that he was plastered in sun cream as his face was getting considerably red. Some of his medication was photo sensitive and meant he would burn pretty easily. I got hold of some Factor 60 before we left for Italy which was for babies and children and it turned out to be a wise choice. I dived in the water; it felt like I was shedding my skin and growing a new skin as the cool temperature spread over my body.

Like parents having to watch their children, I kept one eye on Sebastian who seemed to be enjoying the moments of calm. I knew I'd never get him in the water but I didn't feel so guilty about leaving him out of it. We must have stayed for over an hour as Sebastian was beginning to get agitated and asking when were we going. I snuck in a few more laps in the pool and then reluctantly got out.

We left the hotel to find somewhere to eat and found a small café in the Piazza San Ambrogo. Of course we tried the ice-cream Italy is so famous for which melted the moment we left the shop but I was very happy that I was getting to utilize my language skills. I was actually more fluent speaking Italian than I thought thanks to Sophia who would sometimes only speak to me in Italian and expect my reply in Italian. Sophia: being here in Italy I had thoughts of us running around in my head. Did part of me still miss her? I remembered the way she would brush up against me, her long legs showing off the pink chiffon dress I bought her, the way she flicked her hair and tossed her head. Did I miss it? Yes. Did I want her back? No.

"So what do you want to do first?"

"Climb the Camponile and the Dome."

"Climb? Can we not just admire it from our feet on the ground perspective?"

"Are you afraid, Benjamin?"

"No," Yes I was, "but it's really hot for so much physical exertion."

"We won't get the best view and it said in the guidebook in the hotel that it was one of the 'primary features of touring Florence' and is not to be missed."

"You really want to don't you?"

"Yes." The campanile, the tower was 85 metres high but had a small lift that went half-way. The Dome on the other hand had a spiral staircase of 464 steps; at least 450 more than I wanted to climb. The views were said to be spectacular but honestly I'd rather see them on a postcard. As the trip was about Sebastian I, of course, conceded. I just hoped that he wouldn't have to phone for an ambulance. "Come on then, let's go."

I felt like I was going to die. It was 100 times worse than the climb up to Sebastian on his college roof. I had great impetus to get up there then, here the impetus for a pretty view wasn't that motivating. However I braved it out, any therapist would have been proud of me. I kept the palm of my hand on the walls and tried to ignore the elevating views as they were passing by me. Sebastian strode on eager to get to the top. What seemed like ten thousand tourists passed by me as I was quietly had a panic attack. I gave up trudging and sat on the step, catching my breath as and when I could. The sweat was just pouring off me. I was a totally knackered 23 year old and I really needed to go to a gym but the thought of embarrassing myself in front of guys with more muscles than Goliath did not appeal to me in the slightest. Susan used to go to a spinning class which I always assumed had something to do with Greeks and the spinning of plates on their heads. Walking the dog was all the exercise we could get now.

After a few minutes rest I ploughed on, children were practically running past me as their exhausted parents looked like I did. Sebastian appeared at the next break point in the steps.

"There's a lift. I found the lift."

"Thank Christ. Did you get to the top and take a photo? We haven't taken many photos have we?"

"Yeah, I got loads, you can see for miles and miles, you should see it. You're very unfit."

"I'm going to take your word for it about the view but can we now go down and where is that bloody lift?"

"It's about 150 steps down from here; I counted them on the way up."

"150 you say? That's just great, bloody great."

He led the way down, I had no idea where he got the energy from; he was hardly eating. I wondered if it was his medication or lack of but I had practically fed his medication to him so he couldn't have been getting more hyper. I just put it down to enthusiasm and prayed that we would reach that lift. Spiral staircases are surprisingly harder to walk down than climb up as your sense of equilibrium is off balance so my hand and sometimes both hands lay firmly on the wall.

Sebastian darted ahead to the lift. The two man lift had an enormous queue which consisted mostly of small Japanese tourists, who could probably fit far more in the lift than permitted, and those inevitable obese Americans, who hadn't died climbing up. It was better to keep moving rather than waiting for nightfall at the lift "Keep going Seb, I'll be right behind you otherwise we'll be here forever if we wait to take this lift." I had no idea how long it took me to reach the safety of the pavement but I wanted to park my sorry, tired ass down on it. The heat was still oppressive but I could feel the faintness of a breeze picking up. After navigating us successfully back to our hotel with my legs no longer felt part of my body we climbed the stairs to our room and I stumbled on what appeared to be nothing. I could not wait to throw myself onto the bed. Stinking sweat was now my constant companion and I recovered sufficiently enough to take a cool shower as Sebastian sat cross legged on the floor flicking the TV remote control from channel to channel; it was even more annoying in a foreign language. "Seb, just choose a channel or turn it off. You need to take a shower."

"No thanks."

"Yes, please. We can't have you stinking up Florence. You either, come and do it yourself; or I'm going to make you. And at this moment I'm tired and irritable." He sulkily came into the bathroom and paused a few moments before removing his clothes. For once I didn't have to push him under the water. He still stood stock still though. "Here; use the soap." I stood at the door half watching him, half closing my eyes for a small rest. He played with the soap a bit but I wasn't in the mood for any arguing or anything that required some sort of physical activity. At least his body saw some water.

As I lay on the bed trying desperately to keep awake, Sebastian returned to his Buddha position on the floor and had found an Italian TV channel to watch. He hadn't dressed but that wasn't really important so I left him to it. I woke what seemed to be a couple of hours later; Sebastian was in exactly the same position. I questioned as to whether he moved at all during that time. He was mumbling a little and giggling at the television but he didn't seem to notice when I turned it off. I felt more refreshed after my nap and was ready once again to face the world.

It was around 8.30 when we left the hotel in search of something to eat. The temperature was cooler and the streets less busy. Just off the Piazza Santa Croce was a small traditional, family run restaurant; it would be the restaurant we would frequently return to during our stay. The tables and chairs were similar to old fashioned benches found in schools and there was no music, just the sound of Italian voices and every so often English chatter. A young woman caught my eye; she had her back to us but she had the most sublime curvy figure and black hair that reached her waist. I was curious and hoped that she would turn around. I stopped for a second; was this not part of my reoccurring dream? She did turn around and she was as lovely from the front. She looked a lot like Sophia but her facial features were more subtle. Sebastian who at first was dissecting the menu looked up and suddenly his face just lit up as if he had seen his most desired thing. As she came across, with notepad in hand to take our order Sebastian grew all shy and looked down at his feet. She was definitely more taken with him. I gave her our order but her smile was for him. He bashfully asked her name and told her she had beautiful hair. She understood a little English and I think she understood him. I'd never seen my brother flirt before and I was rather fascinated by it. Here was someone whose world was a huge mystery to me and the subject of girls had never been a hot topic with him. He seemed not hampered by his scarring and appeared genuinely interested in her. Her name was Alessa and it was her family that ran the restaurant.

"Are you flirting with her?" I thought I saw a cheeky smile cross his face. "She's very pretty."

"Prettier than Sarah?"

"Definitely prettier than Sarah."

"Do you think she'll go on a date with me?"

"That maybe a little premature; perhaps just chat to her as she may have a boyfriend. I'm in no fit state to be used as a punch bag for jealous partners."

When she bought our meal Sebastian just stared at her as if mesmerised. I gave him a small kick under the table to break his unwavering concentration which jolted him back into life. He talked about her incessantly through the meal; I'd never known him to be like this. Granted his comments weren't all appropriate or even relevant but he seemed genuine enough. Half way through our meal Alessa brought her father over to meet us who welcomed us to his restaurant and to Florence. He was a large rotund and jolly man whose size really indicated his love of food. He had only ever been to London once as a small child as his father, long since deceased, was British. His mother was in her nineties now and lived at the family vineyard on the outskirts of Florence. He generously invited us to spend a day with his family there as they closed the restaurant on Sundays. I graciously accepted their offer knowing that Sebastian would have irritated me all night had I not. The flirting continued between Alessa and Sebastian and perhaps unfairly I was waiting for the penny to drop in regards to Sebastian's unusual demeanour. The evening was a highlight, the food was good, the company great and Alessa's mother's singing was truly enchanting. It was around 1am when we left and yes I admit I had had several glasses of wine.

That evening I finally saw my brother's personality prior to his illness, he was funny, kind and gentle but he was also vulnerable to the opposite sex. As far as I was aware he had not had any relationship or even a date with any girl and I hoped, even this sweet holiday 'love' would not harm him or his recovery. I giddily walked back to the hotel with Sebastian lingering behind. That night he slept on the floor, curled up like a dog at my feet.

XX

The hangover was torturous, my was head pounding, my mouth was so dry it was like trying to chew flour and I had the uneasiness and fragile state of my stomach. I had gone to bed with my clothes on and needed the shock of a shower to shake some sense into me. I would have liked to have gone for a swim but I wasn't going to make the mistake of leaving him again.

Sebastian's mood had taken a turn for the worst when I woke him up. He refused point blank to get up and dress and instead jumped on the bed and straight under the covers and I heard him mumbling something about God. I knew for a fact that I gave him his meds when we returned from the restaurant but there was nothing more I could do than to start searching to see if he had been hoarding or spitting them out. I knew I should have checked that he'd swallowed them on our return but I can't remember exactly the point when I passed out. Sure enough in the bathroom bin were four tablets.

"Why did you spit out your meds, Seb? You've taken them up to now?"

"I don't need them; I don't want to be poisoned before I see Alessa again."

I was tired of this game now and repeating myself more times than a parrot. "When we left home you promised me you would take them and I think you need to fulfil your end of the bargain." I was getting frustrated talking to a duvet so grabbed it hard and threw it on the floor, "If you don't take them now we're going home and you won't see Alessa, it is your choice."

Of course he came round, I didn't like to threaten him but it was going to be my weapon in the war of medication of the next few days. He compliantly changed and washed; well I say washed, it could be loosely described as 'water lightly touched face'. It was another day of searing heat and Sebastian had the initial stages of sun burn on his arms, our small bottle of sun cream was rapidly running out and we ended up buying more sun cream than bottles of water.

The Uffizi Gallery has the most comprehensive collection of Renaissance art in the world and the last time I visited, with Sophia, we languidly walked the corridors and vast numbers of rooms breathing in the Caravaggio's and Michelangelo's. This time I thought it would be a shorter visit and not as calming but I couldn't have been more wrong as my brother came alive and showed an extraordinary gift for remembering facts and interpreting the masters from his unique point of view.

The wait in the queue to get tickets was an agonising hour but the queue was thankfully in the shade. Sebastian was growing more irritable by the second especially towards the half hour mark. We also had to contend with the stares and gawping at Sebastian as he sat on the step, occasionally giggling to himself. I was so far removed from being affected by it that I just didn't hear it anymore but the physical gap between us and the people behind grew bigger, as they witnessed his odd behaviour. His fringe often covered the scarring but due to the heat he constantly ran his fingers through his hair. I always naively believed he never really saw the discrimination but he did. Once inside the hordes of people dissipated into small groups meandering in every direction. I focused on viewing Sebastian's favourite artists first and anytime left we could wander wherever our feet took us. Although he most favoured modern artists he also had a strong passion for the renaissance like me, his religious proclivity leaning that way anyway. One aspect of the visit I loved: the cool temperature.

Sebastian's usual lethargy when out and about had changed dramatically on this trip; first he raced up the steps at the Dome and now he powered ahead leaving me to quickly pick up the pace behind him. He paused longer in some rooms, standing up close to the painting scrutinizing the work, and in others he took a step in and hastily made a quick exit.

He stopped abruptly in Room 15 which housed Da Vinci, Perugino and Verrocchio. His eyes were intensely focused on Verrocchio's 'The Baptism of Christ.' "That's the picture you had on your wall wasn't it?"

"Yes, the cleansing of Christ, like we all should be. See how the angels bow before him? That's what I want to be. The Bible tells us that we cannot enter the kingdom of heaven with wealth but also you cannot enter with a tarnished unclean soul. There are two conflicting entities of God, those in the walls and those in the sky and you must escape those in the walls to become cleansed and pure. My soul and your soul are not safe, we have to truly believe that innocence and purity will save you. Leonardo Da Vinci was Verrocchio's master and it was he who painted the angels." I was disturbed by his thoughts, before me was a painting of sublime colour, detail and method of brush but he interpreted as a cleansing not only of body but also the soul. "So I need to be cleansed?"

"Oh yes, but you may be saved. I can save you because when I become an angel I can help you cleanse your demons."

This painting held so much meaning to him that I was fascinated with how he disseminated the information before him. He knows he can't be pure because of the demons, his demons, within the walls. They chase him wherever he goes and he is desperate to be free of them. Schizophrenia is such an amalgamation of symptoms and signs that deciphering his true beliefs from his false beliefs, fact from fantasy, is too complex an issue to truly process. I saw beauty in this painting but he saw his destiny. I began to slowly understand my brother's state of mind and how he coped with that broken mind. This trip was an emotional and psychological journey for me, not just for him, and I was so grateful that I was finally able to see how Sebastian saw the world. We must have stayed focused on that Verrocchio for 30 minutes at least. I withdrew studying it after a few minutes so sat back on the cold marble seats in the middle of the room, enjoying the break and left Sebastian to undo its wonders further.

We moved on and paused at the next painting, a De Vinci.

"He was a genius, Ben. He was a botanist, scientist, mathematician, architect and sculptor as well as painter. He had loads of little people working in his head, in each part of his brain. He was born at 10.30pm but in the fifteenth century it would have been called 3 o'clock at night which proves my theory of the non-existence of time. Do you know that he tried to make lizards fly by attaching homemade wings to their bodies?"

"Didn't he design the first helicopter?"

"In 1493, not really designed it but drew the earliest plans of it using spirals and screws. He was trying to reproduce angels. People always assume that angels are female but they are not. Males have larger wings than females. Angels' wings are not on their backs but on their sides like birds."

"So do they look like humans?"

"No they are streams of light and you can only see their face when they are face to face with you. They can go anywhere they wish."

"So you are just waiting for them?"

"Of course and they will come for me. Those people looking at me today they don't realise who I am and that I am someone special. Those supposed doctors, they don't know anything about me and who I am; they just want to poison me with drugs to change my mind. I can see as much with one eye as they can see with two."

"Hungry?" We stopped for lunch in the overpriced café and continued on our art tour. Next was Room 24, a favourite of mine. Known as the Cabinet of Miniatures, it is comprised of a very small room containing around 400 exquisite miniatures. Sebastian wasn't interested so it was a very brief visit. Velazquez was a favourite painter of Sebs as dwarves were featured heavily in his work. Rather than being grotesque, deformed dwarves, seen as a side show in many countries at that time they were an integrated part of the work. Seb was interested, for lack of a better word, in pictures of religion, death, dying and deformity, even in his everyday thinking. Renaissance painting is religion.

After three hours I decided to call it a day, Sebastian was becoming even more introspective and I didn't want to further influence his obsession of religion and death. I had avoided the more disturbing those works of art for that very reason. He continued to mutter and giggle his way to the exit and cause some children to laugh and point at him but he appeared not to notice. As we stepped outside the heat hit me like I'd walked into a sauna with my clothes on and it caused me to stumble a little and

I put my hand out to guide me to the top of the steps. My body was suffering in the heat, I wasn't overweight but big boned shall we say. I recovered sufficiently after a few minutes and made our way over to an ice cream vendor. It melted over our hands in a couple of seconds. Sebastian still hadn't settled and the giggling and muttering hadn't lessened. It seemed like he hadn't even stopped to take a breath and after every few minutes would point to something and laugh. I was just glad that those voices in his head were comforting rather than disturbing. Perhaps I'd made the mistake of taking him to the gallery but I just thought perhaps he was just a little overwhelmed by it all.

We took the path by the river to walk back to the hotel. The responding to voices worsened and it was hard to hold a basic conversation with him. I navigated our way through the cobbled, busy streets, to the hotel and I went for the emergency plan. I crushed two clonazepam into a glass of water and encouraged him to drink it by saying it was just water that he needed to replace any lost fluids from the heat. The pills would provide at least 4 hours of sedation, possibly more, as I desperately needed a break from him even if it was for just half an hour. The swimming pool was calling me so I could clear my head. I left the room only when I was absolutely sure that he was asleep.

Bliss. It was just me in pool and a lonely hotel worker milling around tidying towels and cleaning up glasses. I was on my twentieth lap when I experienced a sharp pain in the side of my head. I clung to the side of the pool until the feeling passed. The hotel worker must have seen me as he came over.

"Permesso signor, stai bene?"

"Va bene, Grazie." My head cleared after a minute or so and I was able to swim to the shallow end to heave myself out. For a moment I thought I was going to pass out. The worker who had seen me struggle came over with a glass of water. I just assumed I had too much sun. "Sono davvero bene grazie." I lay down on one of the sun loungers and closed my eyes.

"Signor! Signor!"

The worker was standing over me.

"Abbiamo bisogno di chuidere."

He was closing the pool. How long had I been asleep? "Che cosa e il tempo?"

"7.00"

"Grazia," I'd been asleep around 4 hours. I leapt off the sun longer, grabbed my shorts and shoes and darted up the stairs in my swimming trunks to the room. I expected the worst: crying, pacing or throwing things in sheer agitation at my disappearance. I flung open the door. He was still asleep, curled up on the bed just where I'd left him. Relieved, I had a cool shower, put on fresh clothes and rang Susan. When Sebastian woke he was rather groggy and I did feel pangs of guilt for deliberately dosing him with sedatives.

We ate at the same restaurant and were as warmly welcomed as if the family had known us for years. Alessa's father Angelo spoke of his father in England and our plans while staying in Florence. Alessa sat next to Sebastian trying to teach him to say hello and goodbye in Italian. I didn't make the mistake again of drinking too much vino although I thought it would be rude if I had not accepted one glass of their vineyard's wine. Alessa's mother sang and danced for the customers and made having a meal there feel like a celebration. I allowed

Sebastian one beer as he was so imprisoned by his medication that I felt he deserved the right to be a normal young man out enjoying himself. He was slowly and positively gradually coming out of that protective shell of his and I wanted him to have fun.

I smiled in amusement as I sat back and watched the most subtle flirting you could ever witness. Both and zAlessa were terribly shy but it strangely wasn't awkward. Something, however, I felt was not quite right with Alessa, she was incredibly pretty but her mannerisms and her innocence came across just like Sebastian's. Her father caught me staring at the pair.

"Lei e lento comprendonio, una ragazza innocente."

Translated it meant that her mind was slow and she was incredibly innocent. "Ha inoltre difficolta." I responded that Sebastian had similar issues too.

"Fa ridere e sorridere."

He said that Sebastian makes her smile and I had the feeling that the feeling was clearly mutual. I made arrangements with Rico that he would pick us up from our hotel at noon and would drive us to the family vineyard just outside the city. It was another late night and we finally stumbled to bed around 1.30 am.

Sebastian was sitting on the balcony when I woke around 8am. I often wondered how he could sit in the same place for hours and not be bored but I guess there was so much going on inside that head of his that there wouldn't be any room for boredom. He wore the same clothes as the previous day and I was in two minds as to whether to let him just stink out Florence or subject him to conformity by making him shower. For the sake of other people's noses and his own comfort I ran the shower. He was certainly getting better at showering and the arguing became less but as I stood at the door there wasn't a lot of washing per se actually taking place. His skin saw water that was all that counted.

We left the hotel and walked into a downpour including a brief show of thunder and lightning. As tourists darted from shelter to shelter we strode out into the piazza. One thing about being British, we are so used to rain. The world doesn't stop when faced with a heavy shower. Within half hour or so the skies cleared and the sun came out to play again. We wandered the back streets where the tourists don't go, taking in the smells from open windows and the hustle and bustle of Italians at work and play. Back on the tourist trail we stopped for an espresso, I now had an inexplicable love for espresso, and to buy some postcards. Sebastian seemed quite mellow and followed wherever I went like an eager puppy.

We passed through Florence's main food market which was worlds away from the local market sellers in London flogging 2lbs of onions for a pound. The fruit and vegetables were huge and the fresh bread smelt divine. Being there bought on the desire for lunch. Sebastian chose where we ate for lunch and we ended up sharing a pizza due to its enormous size. Sebastian was keen to see the statue of David which was housed in the Galleria dell'Accademia. If you were unlucky you would have to join a queue longer than that of the Uffizi for admission. Luckily for us the heavens opened again which drove half of the queue away searching for cover.

A replica of the statue can be seen in the Piazza Vecchio but the original is a sight to behold. It stands around 17ft tall and is probably one of Michelangelo most famous sculptures depicting David of David and Goliath. It was carved out of one block of marble and is an impressive testament to his skills as a sculptor. Sebastian was the first to remark on the difference.

"I thought David was supposed to be a boy not a grown man."

"He was and wasn't particularly ripped like our friend here. Can you imagine if I'd taken up sculpture?"

"David would have looked like Mr Potato Head."

"So I admit it's not my strong point. Remember when you made Mum and Dad that frog in pottery class at school and they thought it was an ashtray?"

"It was definitely a frog, it had legs and eyes."

He started to laugh, a genuine laugh. His laughing started me laughing. God know what other tourists must have thought seeing us beside the statue in fits of the giggles. As he was in a good place emotionally I asked over lunch about the angels in his head. "What do they say to you?

"Things."

"What sort of things? Nice things?"

"They sometimes tell me jokes."

"Jokes? They tell you jokes?"

"Don't be so surprised Benjamin, they do have a sense of humour."

"Can you share one with me?"

"Oh no, it's just between me and them. You have to want to become an angel."

"And they are always nice?"

"Sometimes they get interrupted at night when the people in the walls make too much noise."

He started to giggle; I assumed the angel had told him a joke. "Where do you want go this afternoon?"

"To see the Masaccio."

Tucked away in a small square was a 15th century church that housed a well-recognised fresco by Masaccio of the Crucifixion. I had written an article for The Guardian newspaper on this work a year ago and I was always moved by it on repeated viewings. I bore in mind the last church visit but took the risk to take him to another church. We were the only tourists in there; the quiet only interrupted by the ringing of the church bell.

"Do you know what the inscription means? 'Io fui gia quell che voi seite quell ch'io sono v oi anco sarcte'"

"What?"

"It means 'I once was what I am now what you are and what I am you shall yet be" The living become dead and then a corpse. Cheery stuff eh?"

"Most inscriptions are in Latin. I didn't like Latin at school. Mr Pye slapped me on the backside with a belt after I said I didn't want to conjugate the verb 'to be'."

"Did you tell mum and dad? You never told me."

"Yes."

"What did they say?"

"Nothing. Dad said I shouldn't have been so cheeky and should have paid more attention."

"Did you?"

"I got an A, didn't I?

"And in everything else."

We moved on, stopping every so often at works that interested us. After another break we walked up to the Giardino Di Boboli, a magnificent garden and, to me, unequalled in Italy. The views from terrace are incredible and thankfully because it was a little cooler it was the perfect time to explore the gardens. At the top end of the garden is a huge fountain which features a large statue of Neptune. As I sat on a bench resting my weary feet Sebastian weaved in and out of the cypress trees like he was a small child, every so often he would look in my direction and point something out that excited him. I wasn't surprised by his interest in nature given our conversations over the last few days; nature was good for him and seemed to settle his mind even for a short period of time. We had hardly taken any photos on our trip and so it came as a nice gesture when a young mother with a baby asked if we would like her to take some photos of us together. It was the first time that Sebastian had been photographed with his scared face. I was nervous to look at them as I didn't know what he reaction might be. As it was there was no reaction.

Visiting the garden was a glorious end to the day made even more so by the ride in a horse and carriage back down to the Piazza Vecchio. My poor legs felt they were still running on a treadmill. I made a decision there and then that I needed to lose a few pounds. Sebastian's energy was boundless and I just stood back and enjoyed it. That evening we ate in the hotel and retired to bed early.

I woke up around 3am; Sebastian was not beside me but on the balcony, fully dressed looking up at the stars.

"Hey, are you going somewhere?"

"I need to get out of here."

"Out of this room or out of Florence?"

"Out of the room. Everyone's talking at me and I can't make out what they are saying or what they want. It's all a muddle and my head hurts so I need to get out."

I did wonder whether he had thought about jumping off the balcony. We were three floors up and luckily probably would not kill him if he did. I could see the distress on his face though, "Are the angels in your head?"

"They're telling me to stay away from the walls."

"Shall we go for a walk? Would that help?" I had no idea of what else to think of doing apart from removing him from the situation.

Florence looked very different at 3-00 in the morning. We encountered only one other person, a drunk, sitting on a church step happily singing to himself. The quiet was welcome but a little unnerving all the same, I expected there to be a sudden loud noise at any moment. I had no idea where we were walking to but we came upon a piazza, not too sure which and sat down on the rim of a fountain.

"Just look at all those stars, Seb?"

"That's Polaris, the north star, which you can navigate from, especially sailors; that's Sirius; that's Arcturus, one of the brightest stars and is about 8.6 light years away."

"Why are you so interested in space and the stars?"

"Because it's infinite, there's no end to what we can learn from the stars."

"Do you think there are other life forms out there?"

"I think it is very naïve to think that we are not. It's faith, faith in thinking that somewhere out there is another you and I sitting watching the stars thinking the same thing. There are parallel universes we don't know about so what makes us believe we are the only ones? It doesn't make sense. People think that life forms cannot exist without oxygen but nature will find its way regardless. Creatures can change sex, like frogs, in order to reproduce. Organisms reproduce in unnatural circumstances and Darwinism will always win: survival of the fittest. Humans are becoming weaker and nature will grow ever stronger. Just as the ice age killed the dinosaur, humans will become extinct and the life cycle will continue. The stars are the audience of our gradual destruction."

"Is that where the angels fit in?"

"Angels are everywhere; they are with us now and completely surround us. See that lamp over there? They are seated on it watching and waiting; waiting for the chosen."

"And God?"

"He has a front row seat to the universe. He sends out his angels to collect the pure and the worthy. Those who aren't go to Satan's basement. I'm always tempted by Satan's people but I will become an angel and be escorted to the kingdom of heaven."

"And me, mum and dad?"

"Mum and Dad will not make it but you can be saved. Why did Mum not visit me in hospital? She just left me there."

"Mum loves you and she didn't want to see you so upset and unwell." This question I was so not expecting and had to think on my feet. The crux of it was that she didn't want to and there was no way I was going to tell him that.

"I wasn't unwell."

"Yes you were and you are still unwell to some extent which is why you take medication."

"It's other people who are not well."

I really felt his conviction that I was just talking a load of bullshit and living in one of his parallel universes. "Look another shooting star and another. It's so beautiful out there and here, if I could live here I would. I can see why you are so fascinated by it." A blinding pain suddenly hit the back of my head which made me wince but it left as fast as it came. We sat for what must have been another half hour on the fountain. Thinking that Sebastian wanted to go as he stood up, I wearily pulled my sorry ass up but he didn't walk on but lay down on the pavement gazing up at the stars. "What are you doing?"

"You can see so much more from this position Benjamin. Lie down."

Reluctantly I did so but he was right. The night sky was perfectly clear of cloud apart from the millions of brilliant stars. "Hey look, a shooting star!" We lay there on the pavement, in silence, looking up at the stars, it reminded me of us on the bed in his bedroom staring at the ceiling at home. I turned my head to look at him. He looked…happy. Despite the unusual circumstances that night I felt a strong connection and it was reluctantly that I stood up. "We must go back to the hotel now otherwise we'll be here till breakfast."

"I might dream."

"A horrible dream?"

"My dream is always the same."

"Yeah, mine too." I then did something I've never done before in my life but it just felt right. I took my brother's hand and held it until we reached the hotel. Maybe it was the European influence or maybe it was just love. I truly loved my brother and gazing at the stars with him lying on a pavement in the middle of Florence I realised that the brother I once knew was never coming back but the one whose hand I held was the one I loved.

He fell asleep pretty quickly on our return to the hotel but I couldn't sleep so I took out my sketchbook and started to draw my sleeping brother, curled up like a puppy. I must have been more tired than I thought as it was soon morning and my sketch book lay beside me and a sharp pencil was pointing in my chest.

XXI

Sunday. Bells were ringing all over the city signalling Mass. I hadn't been to Mass in years and for once a part of me felt guilty about it although confessing my sins would be pointless as I lived in sin with a divorced woman, more than a decade older than me and who had given birth to my child. Ten Hail Mary's wouldn't even cover it. Alessa's brother Rico would pick us up at midday so we spent a leisurely morning by the pool. As I performed my laps I could see Sebastian hovering his foot over the water in the shallow end. Well it wasn't so much a whole foot but a few toes at least. No persuasion by me would actually get him to submerge them.

By 12.30 we were heading out of Florence in a black Fiat Panda. Both Sebastian and I were over six foot and so it was a tight uncomfortable squeeze fitting both of us in the back. Undoubtedly the car had seen many years of wear and tear and perhaps an accident or two. The air conditioning was the open windows which of course we then had to shut because of Sebastian's 'allergy' to fresh air against his face; so once again I felt I was in a sauna. The journey took us through tree-lined roads, villages perched on hills surrounded by cypress trees and past vast vineyards of the Mugello Valley. Photographs and sketches I'd done on previous visits never do justice of this incredible natural beauty. I was in awe as we approached a dirt track with vines either side leading up to the family's villa. The shadows from the cypress trees were almost magical. Rico saw my face and smiled.

"Spero che hai fame?"

We were hungry and the car journey was over an hour. I was looking forward to traditional family cooking: "Estremante." I was growing so much more confident in my speaking in Italian, Sophia demanding I speak to her in Italian frequently at home was paying dividends. I was not even conscious that I was doing correctly as it flowed so naturally.

We had a welcome like no other; there must have been three generations of family hugging and kissing us like they'd known us for years. Given Sebastian's reservation about physical contact he showed surprising tolerance. Alessa's grandmother was a small sprightly woman of 93 with mind and body still functioning extremely well. Copious amounts of wine and good food had seen her through the years. Alessa had two sisters and two brothers, all older than she, and both her sisters had children. Crudely put they certainly paid attention to the Pope and Roman Catholic teachings about sex. The love that radiated from this family threw our parents and our other family members into the dust. Here we were fussed over, spoilt with gifts and ploughed with copious amounts of food and their own wine.

Real Italian food cooked from a family kitchen tastes divine; there is no fuss, just honest recipes that have been used for generations. My wine glass was never empty but I kept a sharp eye out on Sebastian's level of drink but after the first half glass he just left others to one side. Alessa now on her home territory was much shyer and at lunch sat beside her grandmother directly opposite Sebastian. Every now and then she would look up and smile sweetly at him. Conversation turned to England, our family and my love life reared its head frequently. I hadn't phoned Susan since yesterday morning and I chastised myself for not doing so last night or this morning. As I watched this family interact did I feel envious? Yes absolutely. The coldness in which we grew up had left its mark on both of us. Here laughs and love were never ever far away.

Alessa's mother, with brother Rico on the piano, burst into vibrant song, it was like watching the beginning of The Godfather movie at the Corleone wedding where the relatives take it in turn to sing to the bride and groom. I was encouraged to join in but I declined. I sang, like all children do, in the school choir but being over 15 years ago I'd just show my lack of musicality and dreadful vocal ability. I did however play the violin for a number of years, very badly I imagine, and it caused a rift between our neighbours as my poor practising skills would last an hour and the dreadful sound I made would float into the neighbours garden and house if they had their windows open. And I also didn't feel like such a cool lad carting that bloody violin around.

After lunch Sebastian stayed at the villa and I was given a tour of the vineyard. I was not prepared for the mammoth tasting session however. Angelo gave me taster after taster of wine and to be honest they all blended into one after three or four. Or it could have been after the ninth or tenth. The effect of the alcohol on my brain affected my power of coherent speech and my previous fluency of Italian took a huge nose dive as I stumbled to find the right words. I'd also forgotten about Sebastian as by now I was back at the villa lost in the song and dance of the Bartolli family and in my drunken state. I remember vividly being waltzed around with Alessa's sister Katarine around the kitchen table. Later, what seemed like more family members and neighbours turned up to join in the festivities I lost count of people after about the twentieth.

It was a long time since I had felt so utterly free and able to make a complete ass out of myself without feeling ashamed or embarrassed. Not since Ibiza with the boys had I let myself dance, definitely not my strong suit, and not felt mortified either post or pre alcohol. Italians sure know how to throw a successful party. I saw Sebastian sitting in the corner with Alessa's and it looked innocent enough. At one point I saw them holding hands but it could have been my drunken state inventing things. At God knows what time in the night we were driven back, yes with an inebriated driver, to the hotel and either the car was spinning around or my head was.

I was so drunk I can't remember even getting in our room. I don't remember getting in bed either; well I didn't quite make it fully to the bed as when I woke I was propped up on my knees beside the bed with half my torso and head on the bed itself. Despite the excess of alcohol whipping around my system I had my reoccurring dream. I'm not a great believer in Freud's dream analysis but I woke up with a surprisingly clear head and clarity and had the strongest desire and urgency to go to Venice. I believed that morning that there had to be a reason for this dream and had to find the answer.

What of Sebastian the previous night? I only remember that they had gone for a walk, chaperoned by Alessa's other sister Maria, in the vineyards and then spent the rest of the evening sitting on a swing outside the villa looking up at the stars.

XXII

Four hours later we were sitting in a café in St Mark's Square, Venice, basking in glorious sunshine. Sebastian had a spring in his step, undoubtedly from the intimate time with Alessa. I promised him faithfully we would drive home via Florence so he could see her again before we left for home. There was a confidence building inside of him that was making this trip even more than just worthwhile. He was becoming a grown up and hopefully a young man who would be able in the future to look after himself and have as much fulfilment as anyone else. He saw something in the square that he wanted to see and wanted to wander around by himself. He was so sure about it that he even asked for some money. I may have been a little too over joyed at this request and could not contain my innate smiling.

I ordered an espresso and sat back to enjoy the hustle and bustle in front of me and the glorious sun. I closed my eyes for what seemed like only a couple of minutes when I felt something soft brush against my hand. I smelt a sweet smell of what seemed like lilies. I opened my eyes, my coffee was in front of me and the waiter or waitress was turning away. I looked back and I saw the figure of a woman walking back inside. She had a shapely figure, long legs shown off by the tightness and shortness of the skirt and had cascading black hair, tied in a loose ponytail with a white ribbon. I shouted 'Grazia,' at her and she turned and flashed me a most beautiful smile.

I began to laugh. Sebastian returned and sat beside me. He began to laugh, a hysterical laugh, laughing I presume at me. It was all just a dream, no horror, no meaning, no hidden messages. We could now return home.

Our mood was buoyant in the car, "So what did you and Alessa get up to while I was getting drunk?"

"Nothing much."

"Nothing much! That's not what I saw. Did you kiss her?"

"Maybe. Just a little bit."

"And?"

"It was nice."

"Very nice?" He was really quite smitten with her and came over all bashful when I questioned him further. I just had to let him see her before we returned home. "So we're heading home now. Did you have fun this week?"

"I think I did."

"That's good enough for me."

We had been on the road a couple of hours when my head started to pound, it was as if there was a boxing match going on inside. I felt nauseous from the pain so I pulled over to the side of the road hoping that a brief rest would help it stop; it reduced a little so I ploughed on. Whenever the opportunity showed itself I would pull over and find a chemist for some pain relief. A few yards ahead the winding road narrowed and climbed a steep incline. All my focus, despite the pounding head, was required to navigate us safely around the bends.

I looked behind at Sebastian's sleeping form on the back seat. A huge smile crossed my face. It had been the most frustrating yet wonderful experience travelling with Sebastian and I felt we had finally connected once again. We had come a long way since that fateful day when he climbed upon that college roof. Although many symptoms still remain he had proved the sceptics wrong that he couldn't cope with normal life. Schizophrenia will never leave him but he is able to sometimes leave it behind to find enjoyment and ultimately love. I discovered how his vulnerable mind worked and how he finds comfort in things that are purely fictional. As for me I would miss Italy but home, with my girlfriend whom I loved and my beautiful son, was where I truly belonged.

After carefully navigating the terrain for a couple of miles I felt a strange sensation, like pins and needles erupting behind my eyes. The stinging turned into burning and an excruciating pain shot into the side of my head. I was no longer in control and within seconds I was driving blind.

XXIII

I open my eyes but there is nothing but black. I'm lying down. I can hear a faint beeping sound. I try to speak but there is something in my throat. My body won't move but I think I can feel something warm resting on one of my hands and feel my fingers being squeezed.

Out of the darkness I hear a faint crying sound which grows louder and louder. It sounds like Susan. It is Susan. I hear a familiar voice; that of my father. I hear my mother's voice also. Where am I? What are they doing here? Are they in my dream?

Images begin to float in front of me. Me, Sebastian and our pony Percy; Granddad reading us ghostly bedtime stories; my first terrifying day at school; John and me cheating on a chemistry exam; Andrew, Harries, George, John and me drunk trying to chat up girls from Essex in Ibiza; George's mum's funeral; Sophia's pink hankie; Susan and Aaron in the rocking chair in Sussex; Sebastian proclaiming he could fly; Sebastian and I lying on the pavement watching the stars. Other images pass but are too quick for me to decipher.

I strain even harder to hear, there is a voice I don't recognise but I hear the words 'brain haemorrhage.' Strange, I don't know anyone who has had a brain haemorrhage...

I realise it's me. I know where I am. I remember a winding hillside road and the blinding pain behind my eyes as I'm driving. Then black. I'm not dead or alive; I'm in limbo and they have all gathered to decide. One of them will have to choose my fate. Will it be my girlfriend who bore my son or my father and mother who gave me life?

Where is my brother? I cannot hear him speak or giggle. Oh God, please tell me that you have saved my brother.

A brilliant shooting star appears in the black and a small light dances towards me. The light hovers inches over me. It is a beautiful face, the face of one of Sebastian's angels. The angel smiles at me, she has the face of perfection, it brings me comfort and its beautiful wings flutter over my hands for a few seconds. She opens her wings and I'm floating into her embrace. I don't feel scared. I feel only my energy slowly slipping away. Sebastian was right. I feel at peace.

A few moments pass and the final sound I hear is the flick of a switch.

EPILOGUE

My dream is always the same. My name is Sebastian,
Benjamin was my brother. I miss him . . .

Lightning Source UK Ltd.
Milton Keynes UK
UKOW051816190712

196282UK00001B/28/P